Christmas *at* Harrington's

Christmas *at* Harrington's

MELODY CARLSON

Revell

a division of Baker Publishing Group
Grand Rapids, Michigan

© 2010 by Melody Carlson

Published by Revell
a division of Baker Publishing Group
P.O. Box 6287, Grand Rapids, MI 49516-6287
www.revellbooks.com

Printed in the United States of America

Library of Congress Cataloging-in-Publication Data
Carlson, Melody.
    Christmas at Harrington's / Melody Carlson.
        p.   cm.
    ISBN 978-0-8007-1925-8 (cloth)
    1. Christmas stories. I. Title.
PS3553.A73257C46 2010
813'.54—dc22   2010016748

Material in chapter 13 taken from 'Twas the Night: The Nativity Story by Melody Carlson, copyright © 2004 by B&H Publishing Group, Nashville, Tennessee. Used by permission.

This book is a work of fiction. Names, characters, places, and incidents are the product of the author's imagination or are used fictitiously. Any resemblance to actual events, locales, or persons, living or dead, is coincidental.

10   11   12   13   14   15   16   7   6   5   4   3   2

The slate-colored sky matched Lena's spirits as she sprinted toward the bus stop. "Don't be late," Mrs. Stanfield had warned earlier. "The bus leaves promptly at 5:15 and there won't be another until tomorrow morning."

Lena hadn't planned to be late. But with two hours to spare, she had ducked into the public library to use the restroom and escape the elements, then found a comfy easy chair. While reading a recipe for cranberry cake in the December issue of *Better Homes and Gardens*, Lena had dozed off, lulled by the warmth, the flickering fluorescent lights, and the sweet, musty smell of books. If not for the librarian's nudge, since the library closed at six, Lena would probably still be sleeping.

Instead, she was running down the sidewalk with the icy wind in her face and her purple parka flapping wildly behind her like a parachute. She waved her arms, calling frantically to the bus driver. "Wait! Please, wait!"

"You were cutting that mighty close," he told her as he opened the door for her. "Hurry up, lady, I've got a schedule to keep."

"Thanks," she gasped breathlessly as she handed him her wrinkled ticket. "I really appreciate—"

"Grab a seat—now." He jerked his thumb backward.

As the bus lurched forward, Lena found an empty pair of seats near the back and quickly ducked in. Scooting next to the window, she clutched her handbag in her lap with trembling hands. That had been close. But she'd made it.

Her stomach rumbled as the bus left the lights of Indianapolis behind. She'd been lucky to snag two seats together. Maybe she could use the space to lie down and really sleep. Except that she was wide awake now. As if on high alert, she watched the bus zip out into the freeway traffic. They were moving so fast that Lena felt dizzy. Was the driver speeding, or was this just one more thing she'd forgotten during her eight years in prison?

Lena tried to peer out the window, but due to the darkness outside and the reading light from the passenger in front of her, all she could see was her own dismal reflection. Pasty round face, weary blue eyes, and dishwater blonde hair in need of attention. She looked away and swallowed hard. Self-pity was something she'd learned to suppress while incarcerated. It served no purpose and could even make an inmate appear weak. And weakness, she'd learned early, was preyed upon. No, she'd quickly decided, bitter was better. And perhaps it would be better here on the outside as well.

"You don't want to return to your hometown?" Mrs. Stanfield, a volunteer social worker, had asked Lena last week. The older woman had been helping make arrangements for Lena's release. Getting out eighteen months early for good behavior had been a bit of a surprise to Lena, although she knew the women's correctional facility was getting crowded, and a number of inmates—some with crimes much more serious than hers—had been paroled. Plus, with Christmas less than four weeks away, perhaps a spirit of goodwill had warmed the hearts of the parole board. Whatever the case, suddenly it was time for Lena to reenter the world at large.

"I want a fresh start in a new town," Lena had firmly told

the volunteer. "Somewhere far away from Willow Creek . . . somewhere outside of Indiana."

Mrs. Stanfield frowned. "But we have a much better success rate for parolees who return to their hometowns and families—it's like a built-in support group."

"Not for me," Lena said. "My parents both passed away while I was in here. There's nothing for me back in Willow Creek." She didn't add that she suspected her parents' illnesses and subsequent deaths, within a year of each other, were partially due to the stress and shame she'd thrust into their otherwise calm and slightly boring lives. They hadn't lasted long enough to hear the truth. Not that they'd been listening—not to Lena anyway.

"So where do you want to go?" Mrs. Stanfield asked with concerned eyes.

"To be honest, I don't really care," Lena admitted.

The social worker shook her head as she studied the paperwork in front of her. "I see here that you're only forty-three." She said this as if forty-three were young. "And you seem intelligent and well-spoken . . . and is it true that you were a pastor's wife?" She looked up with raised brows.

Lena sighed, averting her eyes until her gaze landed on a faded poster about STDs that was hanging lopsided on the bulletin board behind Mrs. Stanfield. The headline read, "What You Don't Know Could Hurt You." Well, that seemed true enough.

Mrs. Stanfield cleared her throat. "Lena?"

"Yes?"

"I was just saying, how about if I put a release package together for you?"

"A release package?"

"Yes. I can choose what I think would be a suitable town for you, make your living arrangements, set up some temporary employment, get your transportation worked out. Would that be acceptable?"

Lena slowly nodded. "I would really appreciate that."

Mrs. Stanfield smiled as she closed the folder. "Then we'll do our best and trust God with the rest. Right?"

"Right." Lena forced a smile, but as she thanked the woman, her voice sounded flat and lifeless to her own ears. When she returned to her cell, she decided not to think about her upcoming release anymore. It wasn't that she wanted to remain in prison. But at the same time, she couldn't imagine life beyond prison. In fact, she couldn't imagine life at all.

Today, when the head matron had handed Lena a rumpled grocery sack of used clothing—which included this ugly purple parka with a broken zipper, a pair of black polyester pants, and a red acrylic turtleneck sweater—Lena had wondered if she'd been naive to allow someone else, even a kindly older lady, to make arrangements for her fate and future.

Now, as the bus sped north into what seemed the heart of this winter storm, Lena clutched the worn handles of the secondhand bag and wondered about the "release package" tucked inside. Was she a fool to have trusted Mrs. Stanfield? But then, naïveté had once been Lena's trademark. Even when her own trustfulness betrayed her and naive innocence deceived her, she still hadn't grasped the magnitude of her own gullibility.

Her stomach growled again, almost as if scolding her for oversleeping in the library. Of course, her laziness had cost her dinner—her just deserts reminded her of her father's "discipline" when she broke his unbendable rules. He would scowl and remind her that "a rod is reserved for the backs of fools."

Lena didn't want to think about that now. Instead she turned on her reading light and opened her oversize handbag. Despite the Ziploc of travel-size personal items and a large envelope that contained her "release package," the bag was mostly empty. And it smelled funny. She extracted the envelope and looked at it. Her future was contained inside this envelope—it would likely be as bland as manila too.

"Your destination is New Haven," the social worker had informed Lena as she met her outside the women's correctional facility earlier that day.

"Connecticut?"

Mrs. Stanfield shook her head. "There are actually a number of New Havens in the country. In this particular New Haven, a small town in northern Minnesota, I happen to have a friend who is willing to give you a job." As she drove Lena into town, she explained that a bus ticket, directions, names, and addresses were enclosed in the envelope. "You will also find a small amount of cash in there," she said before she dropped Lena off. "But you'll have to be extremely frugal until payday."

As it turned out, Lena had already been frugal by forgetting to purchase tonight's dinner. She flipped through the small stack of bills. Two twenties, one ten, two fives, and five ones—a total of sixty-five dollars to last . . . how long? She tucked the cash into a zippered pocket and decided not to think about this either. So much *not* to think about. She vaguely wondered if the brain used more storage to repress memories than to remember them. She knew it took more energy.

"Excuse me, do you mind if I sit here?"

Lena looked up to see an elderly woman peering down at her. She had on a scarlet coat with white fur on the collar and cuffs—very Christmassy in an odd Santa sort of way. Although it looked warm.

"I, uh, no . . . I guess not." Lena reluctantly moved closer to the window. If she'd been honest, she would've told this woman that she did indeed mind—that this seat was hers and to just move on, thank you very much. Before doing time, Lena had considered herself to be scrupulously truthful. The kind of person who followed the rules. She corrected a cashier if she received too much change, never sneaked into a movie, and always waited when the sign said "Don't Walk." Almost painfully honest. But prison had taught her how and when to lie. Nearly always for the sake of self-preservation. Now she wondered if it would be a hard habit to break—or perhaps a habit to hold on to.

The old woman sighed as she eased herself into the other seat. "I always feel that two women traveling alone are safer when they pair up. My name is Moira Phillips." She stuck out a gloved hand.

"I'm Lena Markham." She gently shook the old woman's gloved hand. The smooth black gloves felt like good leather, soft and gently worn.

"Lena." Moira smiled. "What a pretty name. I'm reminded of the exquisite Lena Horne. Did your parents name you after her?"

"Actually, it's short for Helena." Lena set her purse between herself and the window as a safety precaution. Not that she actually thought this old woman was a thief, but she just didn't know. Cautious paranoia was another thing prison had taught her.

"Helena is a lovely name too. But that Lena Horne . . . oh my, what a voice she had, and such a beautiful woman too. I saw all her movies when I was a girl. I just adored her. Goodness, I haven't thought of her in years. Have you seen any of her films?"

"I'm not sure."

"Of course, she was long before your time. But she was exquisite." Moira prattled on about some of the Lena Horne movies she recalled and which ones she had liked best or had seen twice. Lena pretended to listen, but mostly she wished she'd had the guts to tell Moira that she was perfectly comfortable traveling alone and wanted these seats for herself. She wondered if it was too late.

"Do you think she's still alive?"

"What?" Lena realized Moira was expecting a response from her.

"Lena Horne. Do you suppose she's still alive?"

"I have no idea."

"She would be rather old though. At least ninety, I'd venture."

Lena shrugged.

Moira attempted to peel off her big red coat and Lena offered a hand. "That's a nice coat," Lena said as she touched the furry cuff. "Is that real fur?"

Moira laughed. "Just rabbit fur. My sister Lucille forced it on me when the weather snapped cold last week and I hadn't packed a warm overcoat. Then she insisted I wear it home today. I'm sure she was only trying to get rid of it since her daughter-in-law gave it to her a few years ago and she never wore it. I only took it to make her happy. Do you really like it?"

"Well, it looks warm anyway. And it's rather festive." Lena glanced at Moira's outfit—a smoky blue tweed pantsuit with a gray turtleneck underneath and a pretty silk scarf tied loosely around her neck. A stylish contrast to the unusual coat.

"So, where are you headed, Lena?"

"New Haven."

"Oh, wonderful! That's my final destination too." She patted Lena's hand as if this somehow connected them. "Are you going there to visit someone for the holidays?"

"No . . . I, uh, I'm actually relocating there."

"You're moving to New Haven?"

Lena nodded. "How about you? Are you visiting someone for the holidays?"

"Oh, no. I was just visiting my sister Lucille over Thanksgiving. I'm on my way home now. I *live* in New Haven."

Lena nodded again. She suddenly felt very tired, and more than ever she wished she had the courage to tell this woman that she really needed these two seats for herself.

"So what made you choose New Haven?" Moira asked with curious eyes. "Do you have relatives or friends there?"

"No. I don't know anyone there."

Moira looked surprised. "No one? Then what made you want to move there? And so close to Christmastime too?"

Lena pressed her lips together. She had a choice to make right now—either tell the truth and risk offending this seemingly nice woman, or concoct a story to make both of them feel better.

"I don't mean to be nosy," Moira said quietly. "It just seems an odd time to be moving, especially when you don't know anyone in town."

Lena took a quick breath. "The truth is I was just released from the women's correctional facility and I figured New Haven was as good a place as any." There, she'd said it.

Moira blinked then slowly nodded as if absorbing this information. "I see."

"My parole came earlier than I expected, and I didn't want to go home. So I'm off to a fresh start in New Haven." Lena forced a weak smile to soften the news.

Moira slowly pushed herself to her feet, and Lena felt certain that her truth tactic had succeeded—who wanted to sit by an ex-con?—but she wasn't sure whether to be happy or sad.

"Can you help me get my bag up there?" Moira pointed to the overhead storage on the opposite side.

"Your bag?" Lena frowned as she stood.

"It's a bit heavy, I'm afraid. And the cold is bothering the arthritis in my elbow."

Lena opened the storage area and waited as Moira pointed out a gray-and-white tapestry bag. "That one right there."

Lena reached up and pulled down the carry-on, holding it out toward Moira. She was curious as to the contents and why Moira suddenly had need of it. Hopefully she wasn't carrying some sort of self-defense weapon in there—something to fend off a dangerous jailbird—although the bus terminal security probably would've noticed that sort of contraband in their scanner.

"Thank you." Moira balanced her bag on the armrest as Lena returned to her seat. To Lena's surprise, instead of scurrying off to a safer spot, Moira sat right back down next to Lena and proceeded to unzip her bag.

Lena pretended to stare out the window, but she was actually watching the reflection of this mysterious old woman as Moira pawed through the contents of her bag. "Ah, here it is." She held up a rumpled brown paper sack.

Lena continued gazing toward the window. Perhaps she should simply excuse herself to the restroom and then find another seat.

"Are you hungry, dear?"

Lena turned and stared at Moira, who held out what looked like a thick, tasty sandwich encased in plastic wrap. "What?"

"My sister wouldn't think of putting me on the bus without enough food for several days." She chuckled. "Lucille is certain the bus could get stuck somewhere and I'd die of starvation. Would you care for a sandwich?"

Lena looked longingly at the neatly wrapped sandwich. The bread appeared to be sourdough and she spied lettuce and tomato peeking out the edges.

"It's turkey from Thanksgiving. And Swiss cheese, I believe she said."

Lena's mouth was literally watering now. Too nervous to

eat lunch at the penitentiary, she hadn't had anything since breakfast, and even then she'd mostly just picked at the luke-warm, lumpy oatmeal. "Thank you," she said as she took the sandwich. "I'm actually pretty hungry."

"I thought you might be." Moira reached into the bag to produce an identical sandwich. "We also have an orange and an apple and some pretzels and a couple of candy bars." She chuckled. "I told Lucille that I couldn't possibly eat all this, but she insisted."

Lena was ashamed of herself as she slowly unwrapped the sandwich. To think that she'd almost shooed Moira away. Here this kind woman was generous enough to share food—really good food too. In fact, if Lena hadn't already given up on old ideals of faith and God's goodness, she might've even wondered if Moira could possibly be an angel in disguise. As it was, she didn't think it likely.

The hissing sound of wheels on wet pavement, the quiet conversations of a few passengers, and the feeling of wholesome food in Lena's stomach eventually lulled her into something that resembled sleep. When she awoke, it seemed that everyone else on the bus was slumbering.

Wide awake now, Lena stared out the window. With the interior of the bus darkened, she could see an occasional set of headlights or taillights moving north or south down the interstate. She wondered why anyone would want to be out on a night like this. She surely wouldn't . . . if she'd had a choice. But like every other part of her life for the past eight years—maybe even before—it seemed that all rights to choose had been stripped from her.

She knew she was partially to blame for this loss of privilege. When one willingly surrenders her rights, she should expect to have things taken from her. Like the time she brought home a stray kitten knowing full well that her father had no tolerance for house pets. What had she expected would happen? When he angrily put the sweet calico into a shoe box, tying a string around the lid to hold it shut, then shoved it into the trunk of his car to transport to the pound, why should she have been surprised? Why should she have bothered to protest? What difference would it have made? And so she hadn't said anything.

"Thank you for being a big girl," her mother had said as she hurried to get dinner started. It seemed clear Mother wanted everything just right before Lena's father returned. "You did the right thing not to be upset over that silly cat, Lena. It will make it easier for everyone."

Lena had nodded and then gone off to her room to cry in private. Later, despite her mother's attempt to smooth things over with meatloaf and baked potatoes, Lena's father had reprimanded her for bringing home a pet without asking first.

"But if I asked first, you would've said no," she explained with seven-year-old logic.

Naturally, that was not what he'd wanted to hear. He took her to her room, where he quoted the Bible to her again—another Old Testament verse about fools and punishment and how they belonged together—then paddled her bottom with the big wooden spoon. Perhaps he was predicting the pattern of her life—the rod for the backs of fools. And perhaps she should've listened better, learned her lessons, and made wiser choices. Or, she wondered . . . perhaps she had listened too well.

Lena closed her eyes as the bus made another scheduled stop. This was her way of appearing to be sleeping just in case Moira woke up and wanted to chat. Lena liked Moira but found it exhausting to make small talk. And she did not want to think either. Or to remember. She wished she were more of a planner—the sort of person who could size up a situation and take control and be rewarded with a good outcome.

But, as Lena had been told more times than she cared to recall, she was more of a reactor. She'd learned early on that it was more prudent to sit back and wait for someone else to jump in and call the shots, and then she could simply follow along a few steps behind. She had always felt that was the safest route. If she didn't make a decision, she wouldn't make a mistake. That way no one, including her father, could blame her.

But even that philosophy had let her down eventually.

"Next stop, New Haven," the bus driver called as he closed the door after the passengers exited.

Moira woke with a start, grabbing Lena's arm with wide eyes. "What-what—did I miss my stop?"

"It's okay," Lena assured her. "He just said that New Haven was the next stop."

Moira sighed. "Oh, what a relief."

"And don't worry," Lena told her. "I'll wake you if you're—"

"Oh, I'm wide awake now," Moira told her as she sat up straighter. "And if that was Wellington, New Haven is less than an hour away." She brightened. "And my son will be there to pick me up. It'll be good to get home." She looked at Lena with concern. "Where will you be staying?"

Lena fumbled to open her purse and retrieve the papers. She turned on the reading light and peered at the writing. "It says Miller House at 318 Alder Street. And there's a phone number too."

Moira nodded in a sober sort of way. "Yes, that's a boarding-house right downtown. Not the nicest part of town, mind you. You make sure you lock your door, dear."

"Thank you, I will."

"And will you look for work somewhere?"

"I'm supposed to report to Harrington's Department Store on Main Street."

"That's wonderful. Camilla Harrington is a good friend of mine. Her family has owned that store for generations, close to a hundred years, I'll bet." Moira's brow creased.

17

"Unfortunately, it doesn't look as if the store will be around for the next hundred years. According to Camilla, they'll be lucky to make it to the end of this year. And that's only if Christmas shoppers loosen their belts."

"Oh?"

"Camilla says the economically hard times have lured even her most faithful customers off to those big discount stores. Consequently, Harrington's is suffering."

"That's too bad." Lena shook her head. *And not just too bad for the department store either*, she thought. Hopefully she'd still have a job by Monday. Mrs. Stanfield had promised Lena that she'd have work there even if it was only through the holidays. After that, Lena would be on her own.

"What sort of work will you be doing at Harrington's?"

"I'm not exactly sure."

"Well, what sort of work did you do . . . before your incarceration?"

Lena thought about this. Should she answer honestly or make something up? She knew from experience in prison that once she started a lie, it was hard to maintain it. Really, in the long run, truth was easier. "Mostly I was a housewife," she said. "And I did some bookkeeping for the church part-time."

Moira's eyebrows arched slightly. "You're married?"

"Not anymore." Lena took in a quick breath.

"But you say you went to church?"

"My husband was a minister." The admission felt like acid on her tongue.

Moira's eyebrows lifted even higher. "A minister?"

Lena nodded then looked down at her hands, clasping them together to keep them from trembling. It was her normal reaction whenever she thought about Daniel. She could tell Moira the whole story about how her husband was a crooked

18

minister, but that might take more time than they had left in this trip. Besides, Lena wasn't sure she wanted that much of her past to follow her to New Haven. After all, this town was supposed to be her fresh start.

"Perhaps Camilla will put you in the bookkeeping department," Moira mused.

Lena considered telling Moira that seemed unlikely considering her conviction, but decided that for her own self-preservation, she should draw the line on giving out too much information. Although Moira seemed like a kind and generous person, Lena had no way of knowing if this woman might be given to gossip. And Lena knew from experience that some of the seemingly nicest people could have the loosest of tongues. Plus Moira had already admitted to being good friends with the woman who would likely be Lena's new boss. That is, if the store was still in business by the time she got there . . . No, Lena decided, sometimes it was better to keep your cards close to your chest.

"Or maybe you'll work in sales . . . ?"

Lena heard the question in Moira's voice and knew she was fishing for more information. "Oh, I don't think sales," Lena said. "I've never done anything like that before."

"Well, I'm sure you and Camilla will figure it all out." Moira patted her hand. "But you mentioned church and I'd like to be the first one to invite you to my church."

"Thank you." Lena forced a smile.

Moira dug in her handbag, finally pulling out a pen and a little notebook. She adjusted her glasses then carefully began to write. "Sunday services are at 10:30." She looked up. "Why, that's tomorrow, isn't it?"

Lena nodded.

"Well, I hope you'll join us." Moira tore off a slip of paper and tucked it into Lena's hand.

"Thank you," Lena said again.

Moira seemed to study her. "And you say your husband is a minister?"

"Was a minister," Lena corrected.

"He's no longer in the ministry?"

Lena scowled. Why had she told Moira that?

"I'm sorry, dear." Moira patted her hand again. "I didn't mean to be nosy. It's just that I can tell you've been through a lot. I only wanted to be friendly."

"That's okay," Lena said quietly. "My husband was *in* the ministry, but he wasn't exactly an ordained minister. Of course, I didn't know that when I married him. It came out later." *Too much later*, she almost added.

"Was he a wolf in sheep's clothing?"

Lena couldn't help but smile at this. "Yes, that's a fairly accurate description of the man."

Moira tsk-tsked. "I'm so sorry for your sake, Lena. I can tell that you're a lovely person and it must've been quite an ordeal that you've been through."

"Really?" Lena asked. "You can tell that just by looking at me?"

Moira nodded. "Oh, yes, it's in your eyes, dear. I knew as soon as I saw you that you were a woman who'd been hurt deeply."

Lena sucked in her breath and looked away.

"And I'm usually right about these things," Moira continued. "I don't mean to brag, but it's kind of like a gift. I have this way of knowing people. Some call it discernment. My son says I'd be useful in selecting jurors." She laughed. "Not that I've ever been involved in that. But there have been times when Sam hinted at it."

"Sam?"

"Oh, my son. He's an attorney."

Lena bristled. Just the word *attorney* made her uneasy. Lena's experiences with attorneys (aka lawyers), DAs, judges, the prosecution, the defense, and the rest of the legal world in general had left her completely distrustful of the entire judicial system. And it was hard to believe that someone as sweet as Moira could have mothered a sleazy lawyer. Still, it seemed unfair to hold it against her.

"Sam has his own firm," Moira said with obvious pride. "And his dream is for his daughter Beth to follow in his footsteps."

"How does his daughter feel about that?" Lena was familiar with pushy fathers. A few daughters, like Lena, caved. But most others, Lena suspected, pushed back.

"Oh, Beth humors him, but I doubt she'll go to law school. She's not like that at all. She's more artistic and creative . . . like her mother."

"How old is Beth?" Lena asked this simply to keep the conversation moving toward less dangerous territory. If she could get Moira going on about her family, they might make it all the way to New Haven without focusing on Lena again.

"Beth turned fourteen in October. Sam, bless his heart, acts as if it's all over now. As if he's losing his little girl. But Beth is a good girl and quite sensible too. I don't think he's got anything to worry about."

Moira continued to sing her granddaughter's praises. "I'd nearly given up on ever having grandchildren," she finally admitted. "We'd had Sam late in life, but I hadn't expected him to follow our lead. But then—surprise—Beth came along and she's been the apple of my eye ever since." Moira paused to take a breath. "But I've been going on and on about me. How about you, dear, do you have any children?"

Lena shook her head.

Moira patted her hand *again*. "Not yet anyway."

Lena shrugged. What was the point of telling this woman that she would never have children? That she'd already spent too much money on infertility treatments? Or that that part of her had died when she was locked up eight years ago?

"Oh, look," Moira said, "we're coming into town."

Lena turned to look out the window. In the dawn's gray light, she could see what looked like an old-fashioned downtown area with brick buildings and iron lampposts that were already decorated with Christmas wreaths and shiny red bows. It really seemed a charming town—like a backdrop in a Norman Rockwell painting. And nothing whatsoever like Lena's hometown of Willow Creek.

"There's Harrington's." Moira pointed to a large brick building with lots of plate-glass windows, all trimmed beautifully for Christmas.

"Very nice," Lena murmured.

"Like any town, New Haven has its problems, but for the most part it's filled with decent, hardworking people."

Lena pressed her lips together. Decent, hardworking . . . not exactly how someone would describe an ex-con. Certainly not how anyone back in Willow Creek would describe Lena now.

"New Haven," the driver called as he pulled to a stop. "All out for New Haven."

"The Miller House is only a few blocks away," Moira said as Lena helped carry her tapestry bag down the aisle. "But I'm sure my son would be happy to give you a lift."

"Thank you," Lena told Moira, "but I'd prefer to walk—stretch my legs a bit and maybe stop for some breakfast."

"If you're sure."

Lena took Moira's arm, helping her down the bus steps. "Yes, thank you."

"Thank *you!*" Moira beamed at Lena. "You made my trip home most pleasant."

Suddenly Lena was curious why someone like Moira—so well-dressed, well-spoken, mother of an attorney—would choose the bus for transportation. But perhaps Moira, like Lena, had her secrets too.

"Mom!" a middle-aged man called from across the street. He waved to Moira as he jogged over, first hugging her then taking the tapestry carry-on bag from Lena while Moira did a quick introduction.

"Lena kept me company all night," Moira told Sam. "She's moving to town."

He gave Lena what seemed a slightly suspicious look then smiled. "Pleased to meet you and welcome to New Haven." He turned to gather up Moira's other suitcase from where the driver had set it on the sidewalk.

"You're sure you don't want a ride?" Moira asked. "It's awfully cold out."

"No, the fresh air feels good," Lena said. "Thanks anyway . . . for everything."

"Remember about church tomorrow," Moira called out as Sam, loaded down with her bags, linked arms with her to cross the street.

"Yes," Lena called back, "I'll remember." She watched as the two slowly made their way across the quiet street to where a silver BMW sedan was parked. Sam helped his mother into the car then put her bags in the trunk, closing it with a solid thunk. Then, as if he knew he was being watched, he turned and stared curiously at Lena.

Embarrassed to be seen spying, she ducked her head against the wind and hurried down the sidewalk. Where she was going, she had no idea. Just away from sweet Moira and her lawyer son. Lena had little tolerance for normal people doing normal things anymore. People who belonged in a world that Lena could barely recall, a world where someone like her would never be welcome.

Hearing the jingle of a bell, Lena noticed a young couple emerging from what appeared to be a small restaurant across the street. The sign said Red Hen Café, and with lights on inside, it appeared to be open. The thought of walking into a restaurant, ordering a cup of coffee with real cream, and just sitting there was suddenly irresistible and almost dreamlike. How long had it been?

As she crossed the street, she felt slightly giddy with anticipation. Perhaps she could order a small breakfast too. Not anything too expensive because she knew she was pinching pennies. But maybe a side order of bacon and an egg.

The bell on the door jingled again as she went in. Met with the sound of Christmas music, warmth, and the smell of good cooking, Lena experienced a strange surge of hope. She was really on the outside—she was free!

"Take whichever table you like," called a woman about Lena's age. "Coffee?"

"Yes," Lena said. "And cream too, please."

"Coming right up."

Lena walked slowly through the restaurant, where most of the tables were vacant, looking carefully before she chose a booth by the window. She set down her purse and removed the awful purple parka, folding it as small as she could before setting it on the other side of the booth, then slid in to sit down.

"Here you go," the woman said as she placed a mug of coffee and a jug of cream on the table. She pulled a menu out from under her elbow.

"Thank you," Lena murmured as she opened the plastic-covered menu. She looked for the breakfast section as the waitress told her this morning's breakfast special of biscuits and gravy before she hurried back to the kitchen to pick up an order. Several minutes passed as Lena pretended to be reading the menu.

"Sorry that took so long," the waitress said as she returned. "We're a little shorthanded. Just lost a waitress yesterday." She jerked her thumb toward the "Help Wanted" sign by the cash register. "Hoping we'll get someone soon. Now, what can I get for you?"

Lena ordered the Little Red Hen, which had two eggs, two strips of bacon, hash browns, and toast—only $3.99, about the same price as two side orders.

"So did I see you getting off the bus this morning?" the waitress asked as she tucked the pencil back behind her ear.

"Uh, yes." Lena studied the woman, wondering why she should care who got on or off the bus.

"I'm not really a busybody," she said quickly.

"That's what you say," called a male voice from back in the kitchen.

"Oh, be quiet, Jimmy." She smiled at Lena. "I just like to pay attention, you know. No harm in that, right?"

"No. It's good to pay attention."

"So are you visiting?"

"Actually I'm moving here."

The woman brightened. "Well, welcome then." She stuck out her hand. "I'm Bonnie Wyler and this is my restaurant."

"I'm Lena Markham." She shook her hand.

"Hey, you're not looking for work, are you?"

"I, uh, I kind of have a job lined up . . . at least I think I do."

"Well, if it doesn't work out and this sign is still up, I'm happy to talk."

"Thank you," Lena said. "I'll keep that in mind." But even as she said it, Lena was doubtful. She'd never waited tables before and wasn't sure she'd be any good at it now.

"The pay's not so great," Bonnie admitted, "but sometimes the tips are okay."

"I'll keep that in mind."

Bonnie nodded then retreated to the kitchen again. Lena wondered if it might actually be fun working at a place like this. It seemed friendly and warm, and at least she'd have something to eat. But as more customers came in, the place got louder and busier. And seeing that Bonnie, who was obviously very experienced, seemed harried and stressed, Lena decided this wouldn't be a good job fit for her.

Lena had always been drawn to peace and quiet and orderliness. Perhaps that's why she took accounting in college. There was comfort in creating tidy columns, organizing spreadsheets, and making sure the numbers added up correctly. It always brought her great satisfaction. It used to, anyway. She wondered what kind of a job they would offer her at the department store.

"Will that be it for you?" Bonnie asked as she picked up Lena's empty plate.

"Yes, thank you. It was very good."

"Thanks." Bonnie set down the bill and cleared the rest of the table as Lena reached for her purse, digging in her small stack of bills to remove a five and a one. "Keep the change," she told Bonnie. It wasn't even a 15 percent tip, but under the circumstances, it would have to do.

"Thanks again." Bonnie nodded. "And remember, if you need a job . . ."

"I will." As Lena put on her purple parka, she wondered if perhaps she might be able to handle a job like this after all. Oh, sure, she'd probably be clumsy at first. But at least she'd be good at tallying up the check and making correct change. Not all waitresses were good at math.

She picked up her purse and headed for the door, pausing to check the clock by the kitchen. It was a quarter to nine now. She had managed to spend nearly an hour here. Perhaps it would be nine by the time she reached the boardinghouse. That seemed a respectable time to inquire about her room.

She headed down Main Street, looking at the addresses of the businesses in hopes that the numbers would help determine which direction to go. She found Alder after four blocks, turned, and continued until she came to Third Street. There on the corner of Third and Alder was a pale pink three-story house with a weathered sign out front that read "Miller House: Rooms for Rent. Weekly and Monthly Rates."

She walked up to the covered front porch. A couple of sagging old sofas were wedged on either side of it, along with some plastic lawn chairs and rickety-looking tables, where several ashtrays overflowed with cigarette butts. It seemed this was the designated smoking area. Hopefully that meant smoking indoors wasn't allowed. Lena had actually taken up smoking for a while in prison. It was her little way of thumbing her nose at the world she'd left behind. But it never really suited her, plus it was expensive.

She wasn't sure whether to knock on the door or just walk in. How did boardinghouses work? Perhaps it was like a hotel. In that case, she figured she should try the door, which was unlocked. She opened it with a creak and slowly walked into the poorly lit foyer, where a couple of frumpy armchairs flanked a small plastic table with some dog-eared magazines on it. The wood flooring looked splintered and worn beyond repair. Miller House had definitely seen better days.

"Looking for someone?"

Lena glanced down the dim hallway to see a guy in a sleeveless gray T-shirt and plaid pajama bottoms coming toward her.

"Are you the manager?"

"Nah, that'd be Lucy." He pointed to a door with a metal "1" on it. "That's her room, but she sleeps kinda late."

"Oh."

He pulled a pack of Camels from his T-shirt pocket and grinned to reveal a broken front tooth. "I'm TJ."

"I, uh, I'm Lena."

"You getting a room here?"

She nodded. "I think so."

"Welcome, then. It's not the Ritz, but hey, it's better than sleeping under a bridge." He chuckled. "Wanna smoke?"

"No thanks."

He nodded. "Yeah, I keep thinking I should quit." Then he shrugged and headed out the front door. She noticed his bare feet and wondered how he could stand out in the cold for long.

"I'm awake now," a woman's voice said.

Lena turned to see a heavyset woman coming from the room. She had on a brown silky robe over a hot pink lacy nightgown. "I'm sorry," Lena said. "Did I wake you?"

"No, TJ's responsible for that. I heard him telling someone that I sleep late, which is true some of the time. But not all of the time." She yawned then stared at Lena. "Who are you anyway?"

Lena dug in her purse to retrieve the letter from Mrs. Stanfield and quickly explained about the arrangements that had been made for her.

"Oh, yeah, you're in room 13. I hope you're not superstitious." Lucy laughed. "And your rent is paid up until the end of December, but I like rent paid at least one week in advance, so that means you'll have to pay me for the first week of January around Christmas. And don't think that just because it's Christmastime I won't remember. Because I will. It's not that I'm a Scrooge, but nobody gets a free ride here. Understand?"

Lena twisted the handle of her purse. "Yes. Of course."

"Good. Now hang on a minute and I'll get your keys and some paperwork."

Lena waited as Lucy went into her room again. She could hear her talking to herself as she rumbled around. "I really need to clean this place up one of these days . . . Now where is that folder?" Finally she emerged with a couple of keys and some papers. "This one is the rules, which I try to keep simple." She handed Lena two printed pages. "And you'll need to fill out the information form. Mostly basic stuff and emergency numbers. It's not like we do references here." She laughed. "No one would tell the truth anyway."

"Right."

Lucy held up a ring with two keys. "The brass one is for the dead bolt in your room, and I strongly recommend you keep it bolted at all times. And the silver key is for the front door, which is supposed to remain locked as well, although some tenants can't seem to remember this rule." She shook her head. "Hence the need to keep your room locked . . . if you get my meaning."

Lena nodded. "I understand."

"I can show you up there if you want." Lucy pointed to the stairs and frowned. "But it's on the third floor and my knees have been giving me trouble and—"

"That's okay," Lena assured her. "I can find it myself."

"And I leave it to the tenants to work out the bathrooms."

Lena frowned. "Work out the bathrooms?"

"You share a bathroom with a few other tenants. Rooms 11, 12, and 14."

"Oh."

"That means you might need to schedule things like showers. Also, the tenants are expected to clean the bathrooms as well as their own rooms. All the cleaning supplies are in the hall closet. I do weekly checks, and it's not like I put on the white gloves, but I won't put up with total slobs either. I leave it up to the tenants to work out the details of whose turn it is to clean the bathroom. Same goes with the kitchen. Mostly I expect folks to clean up their own messes, and if I catch someone who doesn't, they get stuck cleaning the whole kitchen. And I'll warn you, even though I tell tenants to plainly mark any food they keep in the fridge, a lot of food snatching goes on around here. Not much I can do about it. Some tenants get mini fridges for their rooms though. Now, any questions?"

Lena thought for a moment. "Are linens provided?"

"There are towels in your room. I encourage tenants to use them more than once to save on water and electricity. But when you need to, you bring them to me and I'll give you clean ones." Lucy pointed to the rule page. "It's all there in the rules."

"Yes, I'm sure it is." Lena smiled. "Thank you."

"I hope you enjoy your stay at Miller House." Lucy did

a mock bow. "Not that you'll be here long. Most people aren't. Although we have several older tenants who seem happy to stick around. Or maybe they can't afford anything else."

Lena nodded.

"One more thing." Lucy scowled as she shook her forefinger at Lena. "It's written in plain black and white on the rule sheet, but for some reason a lot of tenants seem to overlook this one."

"What's that?"

"No cooking in your room." Lucy leaned forward until her nose was inches from Lena's. "Understand?"

Lena blinked and backed up. "Yes. No cooking in my room."

"That means no hot plates. No microwaves. No toasters. No crock-pots. No toaster ovens. No electric teapots. No electrical appliances—period." Lucy rolled her eyes dramatically. "Besides blowing out the electrical fuses, this place could be a real firetrap. So I will absolutely enforce this rule. Anyone who breaks it will be thrown out. Got it?"

"Yes. I got it."

"Good." Lucy smiled. "Sorry to be so hard-nosed, but I've found it's better to make myself perfectly clear right from the get-go."

"I understand." Lena smiled back. "I can imagine it'd be a big responsibility running a place like this."

"It is." Lucy sighed. "And it's a mostly thankless job too."

"Well, thank you then."

Lucy pulled her robe more tightly around her. "I think you'll be a good tenant, Lena. Let me know if you need anything."

Lena told her she would, but she had a feeling that she'd rather lay low than trouble Lucy for much. Not that Lucy didn't seem like a nice person. She just seemed like someone who didn't want to be bothered.

The steps creaked as Lena went up. She counted each step. It was an old habit, perhaps stemming from her love of numbers, or maybe it was just her way to comfort herself. But she'd been counting things like steps since childhood. Twelve steps, then a landing and a turn, then twelve more. Twenty-four steps. If there ever was a fire from a tenant cooking in their room or the electricity went out, she would know how to count her way down to escape.

Room 13 was the second on the left. She tried the key and was relieved to see that it worked. The door creaked, and she stepped into a sparsely furnished room with a twin bed, bedside table, dresser, and chair. The smell was musty and the chill in the air suggested that it had been unoccupied for a while. She looked across the brown linoleum floor to spot a closed heat vent in the floor. She opened it and warm air began radiating up.

She went over and sat on the bed, testing it to discover that the mattress was thin and the box springs were squeaky. Still, it was a huge improvement over her accommodations for the past eight years. In fact, the whole room was a pleasant surprise. Her own dresser for her things—not that she had any. Her own chair to sit in and just think. Her own bedside table with a lamp she could turn on and off whenever she liked. She could read in the middle of the night if she wanted. Really, the room was perfect.

She stood and went to the window, pulling up the blind to peer outside. The window was murky, obscured by layers of grime, so she used her palm to clear a spot and then peered down into the yards of neighboring homes. From this vantage point, they all seemed carefully aligned with straight fences separating lots. Some backyards had signs of children with swing sets, sandboxes, and toys. Some appeared to have dogs. A few had fruit trees and dormant gardens, which probably looked pretty in summer. But for the most part the yards and homes all looked neat and orderly, giving the impression that life was still relatively good for middle-class America in New Haven.

She sighed, suppressing the small surge of jealousy burning inside her chest. What was it to her if other people were happy? Why shouldn't she be glad for them? She pulled down the shade, slipped off her shoes, and crawled into the squeaky bed. Exhausted from the long bus ride, she was more than ready for some real sleep. All she wanted was to snuggle down for a long winter's nap.

Naturally, the old Christmas rhyme *'Twas the Night Before Christmas* was stuck in her head now. She pulled the thin blankets and bedspread more snugly around her shoulders as she silently began to recite the familiar words of the children's poem. She knew it by heart. As a child, whenever Christmas Eve came, Lena had nagged her mother to read it to her. Mother would wait until Father was distracted, then she and Lena would slip away—out of his earshot since he didn't approve of such ungodly practices. Lena would curl up beside her mother and stare in wonder at the faded illustrations of the old picture book as she listened to her mother's lilting voice read the magical story.

As Lena was drifting to sleep, she wondered what had become of that old book. Probably sold at one of her parents' yard sales or donated to the church's mission fund, like she'd heard everything else had been after the deaths of her parents. Really, that seemed only fair, considering what had been taken. She had no doubts that her parents, particularly her father, had felt partially to blame for everything. And maybe they were.

CHAPTER
4

Lena didn't emerge from her room until one that afternoon. She could've slept longer but was worried she might end up sleeping all day and then be awake all night. Sleepless nights weren't unusual in prison, but here on the outside she wanted to get back to normal hours. And maybe even some other kinds of normal too . . . if that was even possible.

Standing in the hallway with a faded pink hand towel hanging over her arm like a formal waiter, she waited while someone else occupied the bathroom. She'd already tried the door to find it locked, and then a woman's voice had snapped, "Just a minute," in an aggravated way. Lena hoped it wasn't rude to wait like this, but she really needed to go. Finally the door opened and a young woman and a small girl stepped out.

The woman eyed Lena with suspicion. "Are you new here?"

She nodded. "I'm Lena. Room 13."

"I'm Sally. Room 11. And this is Jemima."

Lena studied the little girl. Her strawberry blonde hair was messy and appeared to need a good shampoo, her Minnie Mouse sweatshirt was dirty, and her worn blue jeans were short enough to reveal a pair of skinny ankles, no socks, and canvas tennis shoes. "Jemima, what an interesting name."

The girl peered at Lena. "You mean like the pancakes?"

"No, I mean that Jemima is a pretty name. How old are you?"

"Six and a half."

Lena smiled at them. "Well, I'm pleased to meet you both." And she actually was pleased, or maybe it was relief, but it felt safer to think a mother and child lived here too.

"So . . . welcome to Miller House," Sally said without enthusiasm.

"Have you been here long?" For some reason, and to her own surprise since she'd been waiting to use the bathroom, Lena wanted to extend this conversation a bit.

"Too long." Sally reached over and slapped Jemima's hand. "Stop picking your nose, you brat!"

"I, uh, I hope I didn't rush you out of the bathroom," Lena said quickly. "I'll only be in there a few minutes if you weren't done yet."

"No, we're done." Sally took Jemima roughly by the upper arm. "And you need to go clean up that mess you made in our room, Pig-Pen."

They went their separate ways, but as Lena used the bathroom, she couldn't get the sad, lost look in Jemima's eyes out of her mind. What was a six-year-old doing in a boardinghouse? And why was her mother so angry? Well, that was probably obvious enough—who wanted to be stuck in a place like this?

As Lena was returning to her room, she could hear sounds of a child crying and suspected it was Jemima. The little girl sounded tired and her mother was probably just cranky. Lena told herself to stay out of it. Really, why should it concern her? Hadn't eight years in prison taught Lena that it was better to ignore things like conflict?

Still, Lena could recall the satisfaction she'd experienced when she'd put together the daycare center at the church all those years ago . . . back in that other life. It had been set up as kind of a relief nursery—a chance for moms to have a break. She remembered the gratitude some of the weary moms had expressed. And the children had enjoyed it too.

But why should any of that matter now? *Just keep walking*, she told herself, *go into your room, close the door, and block it all out.*

Instead, she found herself knocking on the door of room 11. "Excuse me," she said when Sally opened the door, "but I used to operate a daycare center in our church and I remembered how moms sometimes need a break. If you'd ever want me to watch Jemima for you, I wouldn't mind."

Sally's brows drew together. "I don't even know you. Why would I let you babysit my child?"

Lena nodded. "I suppose that makes sense. I just thought I'd offer. I'm sorry if I—"

"I want her to babysit me." Jemima poked her head out from behind Sally. "Even though I'm *not* a baby."

Sally frowned at her daughter then narrowed her eyes at Lena. "Fine. I'll think about it. Maybe some other time."

"Okay then." Lena stepped back. "But I'll be going to work on Monday and I'm not sure what my hours—"

"Where are you working?" Sally asked with hungry eyes.

"At Harrington's Department Store."

Sally seemed to assess Lena's lackluster outfit of second-hand clothes then shook her head. "You gotta be kidding. I went in to fill out an application at Harrington's just last week, and those snobs wouldn't even give me the time of day."

"Well, my job was arranged by someone else."

"Lucky for you." Sally sounded spiteful. "Must be nice."

Lena ignored her tone. "Are you looking for work?"

"Like it does me any good."

"The Red Hen Café is hiring."

"Seriously?" Her eyes flickered with hope. "How do you know?"

"I had breakfast there this morning. The owner told me herself. One of the waitresses left just yesterday."

"You know the owner?"

"I only met her today. Her name is Bonnie and she seems nice."

"I have worked in a restaurant before," Sally said.

"You should run down there and talk to her."

Sally looked at Jemima. "But what about—"

"She can stay with me . . . if you want."

She seemed torn.

"I understand your concern," Lena said. "Normally I would agree with you. You should never leave a child with a stranger. But honestly, you can trust me."

Sally pressed her lips together.

"It's okay, Mommy," Jemima assured her. "I like Lena."

"Okay." Sally leaned forward to peer into Lena's eyes. "But if anything goes wrong—"

"Just go, Mommy," Jemima insisted. "Go see about the job before someone else gets it."

Lena nodded. "Your daughter has a good head on her shoulders."

"Just let me fix up a little." Sally glanced down at her green sweatpants with a hole in one knee. "Maybe Jemima can stay with you while I clean up."

"That's fine," Lena said. "And if you'd like, I can take Jemima downstairs and stay in the waiting area while you're over there talking to Bonnie."

Sally seemed to consider this then shook her head. "No, Lucy doesn't like kids hanging around down there. It bugs her. But maybe you and Jemima could stay in my room. That might be better."

"Okay."

"Give us ten minutes," Sally said as she tugged Jemima back to her room. "I'll knock on your door."

Lena nodded then went back to her room. What was she thinking? What was she getting herself into? She sat down on the chair and shook her head. Here she could barely take care of herself and suddenly she was offering to help someone else. It seemed that old habits really did die hard.

In less than ten minutes she heard a knock. When she opened the door, Sally stood there looking much better. "Is it okay if I tell Bonnie that you told me about the job?" she asked Lena as she brushed some lint off of her blazer. "Kind of like a recommendation?"

"It's fine with me, but I doubt it'll help much. I really don't know Bonnie."

Sally peered over Lena's shoulder into her room. "Wow, it's nice and clean in here. Didn't you bring anything?"

"I didn't really have anything to bring."

Sally frowned. "Well, come on over to my room. It's a mess, but at least Jemima has a few things to play with in there."

Lena locked her door and followed Sally into a room that looked just like hers except for an extra rollaway bed and the fact that it really was messy. And smelly like dirty laundry.

"Welcome to the palace," Sally said. "Make sure you lock the door after I leave." She did a quick check in the foggy mirror above the dresser then hurried out. Jemima locked the door behind her.

Lena picked the discarded green sweats off the chair and sat down. "Looks like you and your mom need to find a Laundromat."

"We can't afford to wash our clothes," Jemima said as she picked up a dirty sock then tossed it toward the closet.

"Well, maybe your mom will get that job."

"I hope so. I'm hungry."

"Did you eat today?"

"Just cereal. No milk."

"Oh. You know, you could wash a few clothes in the bathroom sink," Lena suggested. "Like socks and underwear. That way you'd have something clean to wear."

"Wash clothes in the bathroom sink?" Jemima looked at Lena like she'd suggested she wash them in a mud puddle.

"I've done it before," Lena said. "It's not hard."

Jemima still looked skeptical.

Lena leaned over and picked up several child-size socks, a couple of T-shirts, some printed underpants, a pair of white tights, and a pink cotton turtleneck. "Come with me and I'll show you."

"We have to lock the door," Jemima reminded her.

"Oh, that's right." Lena frowned. "I forgot."

"But I have my own key," Jemima said. "Now don't look and I'll get it from my secret hiding place."

Lena turned her back, and Jemima locked the door and followed her to the bathroom. Lena put a stopper in the old sink then turned on the tap. "It helps to use hot water," she explained as she dropped the socks and underwear into the half-filled sink then pushed up her sleeves. She picked up the bar of soap and one sock and began lathering it up and rinsing it until finally it looked almost perfectly clean. She held it up. "See?"

Jemima nodded. "Can I do one?"

"Sure." Feeling a bit like Tom Sawyer whitewashing the fence, Lena handed her the soap and stepped back. Soon Jemima was washing her own socks. Lena left the bathroom door open in case another tenant needed to use the facilities. She stood nearby Jemima, coaching her through the rest of the items, showing her how to rinse the soap out with the tap water and how to wring the clothes. Finally, when everything was washed, they emptied the sink and wiped off droplets of water with a rag Lena found in the cleaning closet.

"But how will we dry them?" Jemima asked as Lena piled the damp items together to take back to the room.

"We'll think of something," Lena said. Before long she'd rigged up a drying station with the chair and hangers arranged over the heating vent in the floor. "They should be dry by this evening," she predicted.

Jemima smiled. "That was fun."

Lena smiled back. "It was fun, wasn't it? We were like pioneers."

"What's a pioneer?"

"People in the olden days. They didn't have washers or dryers or electricity. They had to do everything by hand. It was hard work."

"I think it sounds like fun."

Just then a key turned in the door and Sally burst in with a big smile on her face. "I got the job!"

Jemima ran to her mom and hugged her. "And I washed clothes."

Sally looked doubtful. "What?"

"Lena showed me how to wash clothes in the bathroom sink. Like pirates."

"Like pioneers," Lena corrected her.

"Yeah, that's what I meant." Jemima pointed to their drying station. "Lena said they'll be dry by tonight."

Sally nodded. "Wow, that's a good idea. Maybe I can wash some things too."

"I'll show you how, Mommy."

Lena smiled as she reached for the door. "Congratulations on the job."

"Bonnie wants me to start right away," she said quickly. "Saturday is their busiest night. And Sunday will be busy too. Do you think you could babysit Jemima some more?"

Lena glanced at Jemima and the little girl nodded eagerly. "If you're sure you trust me."

"Hey, you helped me get a job and you taught Jemima how to do laundry. That's more than my own mom ever did for me."

"Then I'm happy to watch Jemima for you."

Sally actually hugged Lena. "Thank you! I'll work until closing—that's nine. And if I'm lucky I'll bring home some tips!"

As quickly as she came, she left, and it was just Lena and Jemima again. "What should we do now?" Jemima asked.

Lena looked around the still messy room. "How about if we clean this place up to surprise your mom when she comes back? We can be pioneer women again."

They worked for about an hour, but Jemima was starting to get tired and Lena remembered that the child hadn't eaten much today. "How about if we get cleaned up and go have some lunch at the Red Hen Café?"

"Where Mommy's working?" Jemima asked with wide eyes.

"Yes, but we won't bother her at work, okay? She needs to do a good job so that Bonnie will want her to keep working there."

"I won't bother her," Jemima promised.

Lena looked at Jemima's messy hair and dirty shirt. "But we should get cleaned up, don't you think? We want to make a good impression on your mom's new boss. Maybe you should take a shower and wash your hair."

"We don't have any shampoo."

"Well, I have some." Lena remembered the little packet of personal items that Mrs. Stanfield had given her. They went to Lena's room for shampoo and a clean towel, and then Lena stood outside the bathroom door, waiting while Jemima showered.

An old man came out of his room with a towel draped over his shoulder and a shaving kit in one hand. "Who are you?" he asked.

"I'm Lena. Room 13."

"I'm Larry Levine. Down the hall." He nodded at the closed bathroom door and rubbed his chin. "Is someone in there?"

"Yes, Jemima's taking a shower."

"You a friend of Sally's?" he asked.

"Yes. We just met, but I'm watching Jemima. Sally got a job today."

"She got a job today?" He looked surprised. "Why, she's been trying for more than two weeks to get one."

Lena explained about the Red Hen Café and Larry seemed genuinely pleased. "Good for Sally. I know she's been flat broke." He lowered his voice. "I even gave her some money for food a couple days ago. But I can't afford to take care of them two. I barely get enough social security to take care of myself."

"I'm done," Jemima announced as she emerged from the bathroom wearing one of her mom's shirts like a bathrobe. That had been Lena's idea.

"Okay, now we better find you something that's somewhat clean to put on." Lena smiled at Larry. "Nice to meet you, Mr. Levine."

"Oh, you can call me Larry. Everyone else does."

Back in the room, Lena told Jemima that they were going to

play treasure hunt and the first one to find the cleanest clothes for Jemima to wear to the Red Hen Café would win.

"What's the prize?" Jemima asked as she went through the various piles of clothing.

"I'm not sure, but I know it'll be good," Lena promised.

"How about this?" Jemima held up a brown corduroy jumper.

"Not bad," Lena said as she shook it out. "But you need something to go under it." She spied a white turtleneck that had a stain right on the front. "How about this?" she asked Jemima.

"It's dirty." She pointed to the spot.

"But that won't show under the jumper. And the sleeves and collar look pretty clean."

"You're right!" Jemima exclaimed. "Are you like magic or something?"

Lena laughed. "How about socks?"

Jemima ran over to the drying station. "Hey, these tights are dry already."

Before long Jemima was neatly dressed, and Lena brushed out her hair and braided it into two neat pigtails. Jemima looked like a completely different girl than when they'd met earlier this afternoon.

"Ready to go?" Lena asked. Soon they both had their coats on and their rooms locked, and they were on their way.

"This is the funnest day I've ever had," Jemima said as she slipped her hand into Lena's.

"The funnest day ever?" Lena asked, even though she knew *funnest* was bad grammar.

"It's the funnest day I've had in a long, long, long time."

"Me too," Lena said with a smile. "And that's the truth."

"What about my prize?" Jemima asked as they were crossing the street to the café.

"After lunch," Lena told her. "I'm hungry."

"Me too."

If Sally was surprised to see them, she didn't show it. "Right this way," she said as she led them to a booth near the back. "How's it going?"

"I'm having the funnest day ever," Jemima said again.

"You and me both." Sally patted the pocket in her red skirt, part of her uniform. "And I even got tips already."

Jemima grinned as she slid onto the red vinyl seat of the booth. "I'm really, really hungry."

Sally winked. "You came to the right place. And you're timing's good too—just between lunch and dinner. Not too busy."

Lena and Jemima both decided to have cheeseburgers and fries and to split a chocolate milkshake. Although Lena knew this wasn't really part of her frugal budget plan, she knew it was what she needed to do. She added up the amount in her head, as well as a ten percent tip, and it came to $15.85, so she rounded it up to sixteen dollars, which meant that her cash had dwindled down to a meager forty-three dollars. Still, there seemed little she could do about it right now.

"All done?" Sally said as she came over and began to clear the table.

"Do you have the check?" Lena asked.

Sally pulled out her pad, tore off the slip of paper, then quickly glanced over her shoulder as she discreetly wadded it up, stuffing it into her pocket. "Thanks," she said. "You girls have a nice day."

Too stunned to respond, Lena stared at Sally as she finished clearing the table and walked away.

"Can we go now?" Jemima seemed oblivious to what her mom had just done—which was probably for the best.

"I, uh, I guess we can go." Lena slowly stood, watching

as Sally returned to the kitchen to pick up another order. Noticing Bonnie at the register, Lena went straight for her. "I'm sorry," she said, "but I think I must've lost the check the waitress put on our table." She fumbled with her purse as if looking for it. "I already tallied it up. Two cheeseburger baskets and one chocolate shake," she said as she set the sixteen dollars on the counter. "Keep the change." Lena noticed Sally watching them from the pass-through in the kitchen. She looked worried.

"Thanks, honey." Bonnie put the cash in the till as Sally emerged with three full plates. "And thanks for sending Sally my way," Bonnie told Lena. "I think she's gonna be a real peach."

"Oh, I'm sure she will be." Lena locked eyes with Sally. "And I don't think you'll be the least bit sorry you hired her." Lena turned back to Bonnie. "By the way, this is Jemima, Sally's daughter."

"Well, aren't you just the cutest little thing," Bonnie leaned over and handed Jemima a red lollipop. "Sally, you didn't tell me you had a little girl."

"Oh?" Sally looked caught off guard as she moved around the end of the counter with the plates. "I thought I mentioned it."

"Well, she's adorable, and as long as she knows how to mind her manners like she did today, she's welcome to visit here from time to time."

Lena waved to Sally. "See you later."

Sally shot Lena a grateful glance as she unloaded the plates in front of three elderly women who were chattering nonstop. "Yeah, later, Lena. Thanks!"

Lena really had no idea what to give Jemima for her surprise, but she told her happy little friend that maybe they'd find it somewhere in town and that it couldn't cost too much. Fortunately, Jemima seemed to understand that money was scarce for a lot of people, not only her mom. So they walked along Main Street, admiring the Christmas decorations and looking in shop windows until Jemima begged to go into the pet shop.

"But you understand we cannot possibly buy a pet of any kind," Lena pointed out.

"I just want to look at the kitties and puppies," Jemima said. "Mommy lets me do that sometimes."

So they went to the back and looked at the puppies and kitties, which might've been dangerous to Lena's budget except that there was no way she could afford any of them. As they were meandering back out, Jemima suddenly stopped and pointed to the large tank of goldfish. "Only twenty-five cents for a goldfish!" she exclaimed. "Can that be my prize, Lena? Please, please, please!"

"Oh, I don't think your mother would—"

"Please, please, please," she begged. "I would take care of it."

Again Lena remembered the time she'd brought home

the kitten . . . and how she'd never even attempted to beg or plead, but had simply given in because that's what she'd been trained to do.

"Please, Lena. I will name her and take care of her and—"

"But a goldfish needs a bowl and food and . . ." Lena gripped the straps of her purse.

"Goldfish are really pretty low maintenance," a young man who was working in the fish area told her. "We've got these bowls on sale for only $2.49 and the fish food's pretty cheap."

"But how do you care for a goldfish?"

"Just feed it daily and change the water about once a week. It's pretty simple."

Now Jemima was begging again.

"Okay," Lena said. "Pick one out, Jemima." She'd already done the math in her head and the whole works was less than five dollars. Still, five dollars out of her steadily shrinking budget meant one less meal. Now she had only thirty-eight dollars and change left . . . and to last her how long? She had to stop spending like this.

With the fish picked out and the food and bowl bagged up and paid for, the young man started to turn off the lights. "We're closing now," he told her. "By the way, make sure you don't put the fish in chlorinated water."

"How do I avoid that?"

"Just fill a pitcher with water and let it sit overnight, and the chlorine will be gone the next day."

She nodded as if this were quite simple. As if she had a pitcher for water in her spartan room. She took Jemima's hand and they hurried back to the boardinghouse.

"What's in the bag?" Lucy asked as they came in.

"A goldfish!" Jemima said.

Lucy shook her head with a sour expression. "We have a no-pets policy."

"It's only a fish," Lena told her. "It'll be confined to a bowl."

"But what if the bowl spills or breaks?"

Lena frowned. "I'll take responsibility for that."

"You will, will you?" Lucy looked skeptical.

"I will."

Lucy rolled her eyes. "I'll hold you to it, Lena."

"Yes, I'm sure you will."

"Okay, here's the deal," Lena said once they were upstairs and Jemima was unlocking the door. "You can keep the fish in your room only if your room is clean."

"Okay," Jemima agreed.

"We need to find a clean, safe place to set the bowl up, and you need to do your part to keep the room clean. Do you understand?"

Jemima nodded.

"And if you don't keep your word, I'll have to move the fish to my room. But you can come visit."

"All right."

"In fact, let's get the fish set up in my room first and then we'll go finish cleaning yours, okay?"

"Sure, that's okay."

They let the fish out of the bag and into the bowl, which looked rather shallow since it was only about a fourth full of water. "I'll go find something to put some more water in," Jemima offered. To Lena's surprise, she quickly returned with a bucket.

"It's from the cleaning closet," Jemima said.

"We better scrub it out really good then," Lena told her, "to make sure there are no cleaning chemicals in it. And we'll leave it in my room tonight just to make sure you don't knock it over. I don't want Lucy throwing me out over spilled water."

It took them several hours to get the room cleaned and

straightened, but as they worked, Lena pieced together the story of why Sally and Jemima were staying in Miller House. "Daddy was mean to Mommy," Jemima told her. "We had to leave really fast one night. All we could take was what Mommy could put in the car before Daddy got home."

"Do you still have the car?"

"No. Mommy had to sell it so we could have money for food and this room. She sold some other stuff too." Jemima frowned. "Like my video player and my DVDs. That made me so mad. But Mommy said we'd have to live on the street without any money." She took in a frightened little breath. "I don't want to live on the street. Mommy showed me where some really poor people live in this yucky alley place. It was scary. One man had black teeth and he looked like a monster." Jemima held her hands up in a scary gesture. "I think he wanted to eat us for dinner."

"How long ago did you come here—I mean to Miller House?"

Jemima shrugged as she struggled to hang a sweater on a hanger. "I don't remember. It was after Halloween though. I remember I got to go trick-or-treating at my old house. I was a princess." She sighed. "But I forgot to bring my princess costume. We had to hurry too fast."

"Oh?"

"I'm not supposed to tell anyone where we came from—I mean the name of our town. And we have different names too." She looked worried. "But you won't tell anyone I said that, will you?"

"No, I won't tell anyone." Lena wondered how many other secrets lurked behind the boardinghouse walls. "Do you go to school?"

"Mommy promised I could go to school after Christmas if she got a job. I'm in first grade and I can already read."

"Do you have any books here?"

Jemima shook her head.

"There's a library in town," Lena said. "Maybe we can go there."

⁂

It was nearly 8:00 when the room was finally straightened. "Wow," Jemima said as she looked around. "Mommy is going to be surprised."

Lena pointed to the spot on the dresser that they'd designated for food, which held a rumpled box of Cheerios, a nearly empty jar of peanut butter, and a small box of crackers. "Do you want something to eat before you go to bed?"

"Is it okay?"

"I don't see why not."

Jemima decided on crackers with peanut butter. "I'll fix them for you," Lena said, "while you put on your pajamas." She pointed to the pink flannel pajamas that she'd laid out on the rollaway bed. She'd unearthed them earlier today and they seemed relatively clean.

"Mommy says it's okay to sleep in my clothes."

"Tonight you're sleeping in your pajamas. And you'll hang up the clothes you wore today." It was strange, she was starting to feel like Mary Poppins. As if any minute she might burst into "A Spoonful of Sugar." Although Miss Poppins's young charges had been spoiled rich kids who ate more than just saltines and peanut butter for dinner.

"What about the goldfish?" Jemima asked after she finished her snack. "The room's clean now."

Lena thought about this. "How about if the goldfish sleeps in my room tonight?"

"Why?"

"Because your mom might come home and not know that

it was there. You know, she could knock it over and spill all the water and break the bowl, and then your poor goldfish would die."

"Oh." Jemima nodded with a serious expression. "Okay."

It was around 8:30 when Lena finally enticed Jemima to get into her bed with the promise of a story. "Do you have a book in your room?" Jemima asked.

"No." Lena shook her head as she sat on the chair.

"Then how can you tell me a story?"

Lena thought about that. "I do know a Christmas story."

"Really?" Jemima sat up with big eyes. "I *love* Christmas stories!"

So for the second time that day, Lena recited *'Twas the Night Before Christmas*. Only this time she did it out loud and with a bit of dramatic flair.

"Wow," Jemima said. "That was really good. Did you make it up?"

"Haven't you ever heard it before?"

"I don't know . . . maybe. Will you tell it again?"

"Perhaps tomorrow night. Now it's time for you to go to sleep. I have big plans for us tomorrow."

"Really?"

Lena nodded as she turned off the light. Sitting there in the darkness, with only a slit of light coming in beneath the closed shade, Lena wondered what kind of big plans she really did have for them tomorrow.

Well, for starters, there was the goldfish. Jemima hadn't decided on a name yet. She was torn between Goldie and Sunshine since the fish was more golden than orange. And Lena had considered a trip to the library, but it would be Sunday so it might not be open.

There was always church . . .

She hadn't forgotten Moira's invitation. But the truth was,

prior to meeting Jemima and Sally, she'd had no intention of putting one foot inside a church again. However, she knew it wouldn't hurt Jemima to attend Sunday school and be with other children. And perhaps it would be a good connection for Sally too. Maybe the church would have some sort of daycare program.

Lena was concerned about who would watch Jemima when both she and Sally were working. That was assuming Lena really would start a job at Harrington's Department Store on Monday. And if not . . . well, she'd just have to cross that bridge later. Good grief, this was only her first day here in New Haven, and already it felt as if she'd been here for days.

But the strangest thing about being here in a different town, sitting in someone else's room, watching someone else's child fall asleep . . . Lena felt more at home than she'd been in years. Even before she'd been sentenced to prison.

Lena woke early the next morning, even before the sun was up. She knew this was mostly due to her inner clock, which was still set on prison time—every day inmates were roused from bed at 6:00 sharp. But today she decided to make the most of it by being the first one to shower. Certainly no one else on their floor would be up this early on a Sunday. Even Sally, who told Lena last night that she was scheduled to work from nine to four, was probably still sleeping.

First she checked on the goldfish—Goldie or Sunshine—and feeling sorry for its shallow pool, she carefully poured in more water from the bucket, filling the bowl to a couple of inches below the top. The fish swam around happily, and Lena took the bucket to the bathroom, dumping the remaining water down the sink before stowing the pail back in the cleaning cupboard.

After her shower, Lena put on the same clothes that she'd worn for two days now. They didn't actually look too bad since she'd laid them out neatly over her chair last night. She was without hangers since she'd donated the ones from her own closet to yesterday's cleanup efforts. But she'd taken the time to pick the balls from the sleeves of the red acrylic sweater, and fortunately, the black polyester pants looked indestructible.

Unfortunately, she'd never cared for synthetic fibers. And she wondered how she was expected to work in a department store with this extremely limited wardrobe. With less than forty dollars to her name, it wasn't as if she could go shopping.

If this was all that released prisoners had to work with after doing time, it was no wonder that some of them went straight back to a life of crime. Not that Lena was tempted to do anything illegal. In fact, she'd never been tempted. She would rather starve and be homeless than steal anything from anyone. And yet she was stuck with a felony record for doing just that.

She removed the slip of paper from the zipper pocket of her purse and unfolded it. Printed neatly on it were the name of Moira's church and the time of the service, as well as Moira's phone number and the words, "Please call me before 9:00 a.m. if you'd like a ride."

Lena had noticed the pay phone downstairs, but suspected it was too early to call Moira since it was still dark out. She wished she had a clock, but she knew Sally did and would come knocking on her door before 8:00. That would give Lena plenty of time—that is, if she really wanted to take Jemima to church.

Lena decided to lie back down on the bed just to think, but the next thing she knew someone was knocking on her door. She realized by the light outside that she must've dozed off. Sally was at her door.

"Jemima is still asleep," Sally said quietly.

"Oh, that's probably good. She seemed tired."

Sally hugged Lena. "I don't know how to thank you. The room was clean. Jemima even has on pajamas. You helped me get that job. You're watching my little girl." She stepped back with teary eyes. "It's like you're my angel."

Lena smiled. "I'm glad I could help."

Sally pulled out some crumpled bills. "It's not much, but I wanted to share some of my tips with you. I wish I could pay you properly for babysitting, but—"

"I don't expect pay." Lena tried to hand the money back to Sally. "And you and Jemima need food and—"

"Bonnie let me bring some food home last night," Sally said as she pushed Lena's hand back. "Just some leftover rolls and pastries she was going to toss. But it's in the room. You and Jemima can have some for breakfast."

"Thank you."

"No, thank *you*. Now I better hurry so I'm not late."

Lena got her purse and the goldfish bowl then locked her door and went over to room 11, where Jemima was just waking up.

"You brought Sunshine!" she exclaimed as she hopped out of the rollaway.

"Sunshine?"

"My goldfish."

"Oh, yes." Lena set the bowl on the dresser. "And Sunshine probably wants some food now." She reminded Jemima how she was supposed to pinch a few flakes like the young man had said and drop them on the surface of the water.

Still wearing her pink pajamas, Jemima quietly stood there watching the fish. "Look," she finally said, "she's eating."

"And you should eat too," Lena told her. "Your mom brought some food from the restaurant last night." She pointed to the paper plate with rolls and pastries.

"Yummy!" Jemima went straight for the cinnamon roll and Lena took a whole wheat roll. She wished she had some milk or fruit or something more nutritious to give to the little girl, but maybe later.

Lena looked at the alarm clock by Sally's unmade bed. "Now, if you wanted, we could probably go to church this—"

"To church?" Jemima exclaimed. "I've always wanted to go to church."

"You mean you've never been?"

She shook her head as she took another bite. "Can we go, please?" she asked with a mouthful.

"Maybe. First you finish that roll, then go wash your hands and get dressed."

While Jemima did this, Lena made Sally's bed. Before long they went down the two flights of stairs and Lena used the pay phone to dial Moira's number. She felt nervous as she waited for it to ring, then suddenly she was talking to Moira.

"Oh, I would love to take you to church with me," Moira chirped.

"And I have a young friend who'd like to come too," Lena said. "Do they have anything for children? Jemima is six years old."

"Jemima can go to Sunday school," Moira told her. "And you can come to the worship service with me."

It was arranged that Lena and Jemima would wait downstairs for Moira to pick them up at 9:30. "I always like to be early," Moira said. "And that will give us time to get Jemima settled in her Sunday school class. Oh, this is delightful, Lena. I'm so glad you called!"

But as Lena and Jemima waited outside on the porch, Lena began to doubt the sensibility of this plan. The last time she'd been in church, Daniel had given the sermon. He'd preached long and hard against idolatry and the worship of material things, and she'd suspected his fiery words were aimed at her. She'd just received an inheritance from her grandmother's estate and wanted to use it for a down payment on a house on Gardenia Lane—a darling little home that she and Daniel would actually own themselves. No more renting. But when he'd heard about it, just days before that sermon, he'd flown into a rage. A real rage.

"Why can't you be satisfied with what you have?" he'd demanded.

"I am satisfied," she said.

"No, you are never satisfied. You always want more. More, more, more."

"More what?"

"When you couldn't have children, you wasted your book-keeping income on those stupid fertility treatments. When the church didn't have a daycare center, you felt it had to have one. Status quo is never good enough for you, Lena. And now you want to buy a house. A house that we can't afford."

"But we can afford it," she said. "With my down payment from Grandma's estate, the monthly payments will be a lot less than rent."

"That's what you think. But there's upkeep and taxes and repairs, and the next thing I know you'll want new furniture."

"But I love our furniture," she assured him. "And owning a home is an investment. Every penny you put into it comes back to you."

He laughed . . . and walked away. "I don't have time for your nonsense," he said. "I need to work on Sunday's sermon."

And Sunday's sermon had been about the love of money and materialism and worshiping graven images like cars, boats, houses . . . By the end of his sermon, Lena had decided that, as usual, Daniel was right. It was wrong for her to want things—especially the sweet little cottage on Gardenia Lane. And it was wrong for her to daydream about the flowers she'd plant out front or the vegetable garden in back, and even more wrong for her to imagine painting her kitchen a nice, warm, buttery yellow. So she'd given in. Just like she'd always done, she'd submitted to the authority of a man who didn't deserve it. And five days later, she'd been arrested for embezzling funds from the church.

"Is that the lady?" Jemima jumped up and ran to the porch railing. "The one who's taking us to church?"

Lena stood and looked out to see a white sedan with a small gray-haired woman at the wheel. "Yes. That's Mrs. Phillips." She grabbed Jemima's hand and hurried over to the car, helping the little girl into the back. "Now buckle up," she told her as she closed the door and got into the passenger's side.

"Good morning," Moira said.

Lena greeted her then introduced her to Jemima.

"It's such a pleasure to take you girls to church with me," she said as she looked both ways then slowly pulled out. "And I know Jemima is going to enjoy Sunday school. The children always seem to have so much fun." She chattered on as she drove less than a mile to the old brick church. "Here we are."

"This is pretty close to Miller House," Lena said as they got out of the car. "I could probably walk here."

"Maybe on a nice warm day. But not today," Moira said. "It's too cold."

Soon they were inside and Moira was guiding them to the children's wing, where she introduced Jemima to Miss Epperson.

"She can call me April," the young woman told Moira. "All the children do." She smiled at Lena. "Are you Jemima's mother?"

"No," Lena said quickly. "Just a friend."

"And what a good friend you are to bring her to church today."

Lena waved goodbye to Jemima, who was already in the classroom and heading straight for what appeared to be some kind of beading project. "I think Jemima's happy to be here," she said to Moira as they headed back down the hallway. "She probably needs to be around kids."

As they walked, Lena told Moira about how Jemima's mother had just found a job. "I'm helping to watch Jemima for now, but I'm supposed to go to work tomorrow. I'm not sure where Jemima will be, and I know how much her mother needs that job."

"Well, perhaps someone here at church can help you with that," Moira said as they entered the sanctuary. "This is where I usually sit." Moira pointed to a pew not far from the front. "Be my guest."

Lena went a ways down the pew and soon they were both seated. "My late husband and I always sat here," Moira said. "His parents had occupied this pew as well." She chuckled. "Now, I don't believe families should own any part of a church, but I suppose I consider this the Phillipses' pew."

"Thank you for sharing it." Lena smiled.

"I do recall that you mentioned your husband had been a minister."

Lena bristled. "Yes. That's true."

"So I imagine you've spent a fair amount of time in church."

Lena nodded.

"Did you miss it while you were . . . away?"

"Not really," she answered. "In fact, I'm still a little surprised to find myself here today."

Moira patted her hand. "I understand."

The sanctuary was beginning to fill up. And it wasn't long until Moira's son, the lawyer, slid in next to his mother, along with a young woman. Or perhaps she was a teenager. Lena couldn't be sure. But, on second glance, the tall, dark-haired girl didn't seem very old.

The organ started playing, and a choir somewhere in the back of the church was singing. Before long, the minister stepped forward and the sermon began.

Fortunately, today's sermon was nothing like the last one Lena had been subjected to. This man spoke in a happy tone and his words were actually encouraging. Although he did talk about hard times and major life challenges, he also made it clear that God was the great provider. He confidently proclaimed how God loved to step in when all else failed. He said that when everything looked hopeless, you could be sure that God was rolling up his sleeves. In fact, it almost seemed that this pleasant-faced minister was talking about Lena's own life. Not that she particularly expected God to do some big miracle for her. But she was open to some kind of help. Wouldn't it be about time?

After the service, Moira made introductions. The young woman turned out to be her granddaughter, Beth. "And you remember my son, Sam, don't you?"

Lena nodded. "Yes. At the bus station."

"I can't believe you took the bus again," Beth said to Moira. "Someday you're going to have to get on a plane, Grandma."

Moira laughed. "Not if I can help it."

"Grandma is terrified of flying," Beth told Lena. "She'd rather ride a bus all night than take a one-hour plane flight." Suddenly the girl looked uncomfortable. "Oh, are you like that too? Is that why you took the bus?"

Lena smiled. "No, I don't have a problem with flying. But the bus was fine too. That's how I met your grandmother, and she even shared her dinner with me."

"I have an idea," Moira said suddenly. "You and little Jemima will come to my house for Sunday dinner today."

"Well, I don't know—"

"I won't take no for an answer."

The idea of a free meal was appealing. "Okay," Lena told her. "We'd love to come."

"Perfect!"

"I should go get Jemima," Lena said. "She won't know where to go."

"Yes, you get her and meet me by the car," Moira said.

Lena explained the invitation to Jemima as they walked out to where the car was parked. "I want you to use your best manners," Lena told her. "Put your napkin in your lap. Don't talk with food in your mouth. That sort of thing."

"Okay." Jemima nodded.

"And remember Mrs. Phillips might have breakable things in her house," Lena continued. "Don't touch anything without asking, okay?"

"I won't."

Soon they were on their way, with Moira chatting happily. "I'm so glad I told Gretchen to make a roast today. I had already invited Sam and Beth over, but I knew there would be far too much food."

"Who's Gretchen?" Jemima asked from the backseat.

"She's my helper and housekeeper."

"Do you have any pets?"

"Just a funny old cat named Edgar Allen."

"Why is he funny?"

Moira laughed. "Oh, he's a bit grumpy and particular."

"What's particular?"

"Maybe you shouldn't ask so many questions," Lena warned Jemima.

"It's okay," Moira assured her. "I love a curious mind." She told Jemima about the old cat that had been fond of her husband before he died several years ago. "Edgar Allen never liked anyone besides Howard. And he's turned into something of a recluse."

"What's a recluse?" Jemima asked as Moira turned into what appeared to be a narrow road but was actually a long, private driveway.

"Someone who keeps to himself," Lena answered for Moira. "A hermit."

"I had a hermit crab once." Jemima told Moira about her crab and how his shell was stinky, and then as they got out of the car, she told her about the goldfish Lena had gotten her. "It was my surprise," she said, "for cleaning my room. Actually, Lena helped me clean my room. But she still got me a surprise. And her name is Sunshine because she's all sunny and yellow. Not orange like most goldfish."

"That sounds very nice," Moira said as she opened a side door to let them in. They went into a large kitchen with lots of windows and dark wood cabinets that were topped in a light-colored stone.

"This is a really nice house," Jemima said. "And it's really pretty too." Her eyes were wide as she looked around. "I never saw a kitchen this big and pretty before."

"Thank you. Sometimes I think it's too big. But when I consider moving . . . well, it just sounds like too much work." Moira led them past a dining area and into a spacious living room. "You make yourselves at home here. Meanwhile I'll hunt down Gretchen and tell her to put a couple more plates on."

With Jemima trailing her, Lena walked through the large room, taking in the gleaming hardwood floors, oriental carpets, antique cabinets, elegant-looking couches and chairs, and even what appeared to be original art on the walls.

"This is a really fancy house," Jemima said quietly.

Lena nodded as she sat on the sofa. It was covered in a tapestry fabric that reminded Lena of the forest with varying shades of green and touches of gold. "Let's sit here," she told Jemima. "And I don't think you should touch anything, okay?"

"Okay." Jemima sat down and primly folded her hands in her lap. "Mrs. Phillips must be really, really rich. Did you ever see a house this fancy before?"

"No, not really." Although in some ways it was similar to her grandmother's house. Oh, larger and more elegant perhaps, but her grandmother had similar tastes, and Lena remembered how she'd always felt like a little princess in that house—when she was allowed to go, which wasn't often. Her father didn't approve of his mother-in-law. He said she was "too worldly."

But at this moment, Lena felt totally out of place, almost like an alien in a foreign land. This home was so vastly different from how she'd lived the past eight years—so beyond her comfort zone. She'd had no idea that the woman she'd met on the bus lived like this.

When she'd first met Moira, Lena assumed she was a widow who lived within her means, riding the bus to save money. But then she'd noticed Moira's nice clothes and thought perhaps her means were not quite so modest. And when she'd seen the lawyer son and his fancy BMW, she grew curious. What kind of well-off son let his mother ride the bus? Then she learned about Moira's fear of flying, and now she didn't know what to think. Except that perhaps it had been a mistake to accept Moira's invitation to Sunday dinner. And yet, it was a free meal.

"Grandma told me to keep you company," Beth said as she entered the living room, tossing her jacket and purse on a chair.

"Oh, we're okay on our own," Lena assured her.

"Okay, I said that all wrong. I *wanted* to come in here and keep you company. Otherwise I'd get stuck peeling potatoes like Dad."

"Your dad's peeling potatoes?" Lena asked.

"He probably wanted to anyway. He likes to tease Gretchen."

"Where's Ed—what's his name again?" Jemima asked Lena.

"Edgar Allen."

"Oh, you mean the cat," Beth said. "Old Edgar Allen is such a grump, I don't think you'd really want to meet him." She sat down in one of the club chairs across from them. "So you must be Jemima."

Jemima nodded with wide eyes. "Who are you?"

"I'm Beth."

"Mrs. Phillips's granddaughter," Lena explained.

"How old are you?" Jemima asked.

"Fourteen."

Jemima looked impressed. "That's pretty old."

"I guess. How old are you?"

"Six and a half."

"That's pretty old too." Beth stood up. "Hey, I have an idea. Do you like toys?"

Jemima's eyes lit up. "Yeah!"

"There's a bunch of my old Barbies and stuff downstairs. We could go play with them if you want."

"Really?" Jemima was already on her feet.

"Sure. Come on." Beth reached for Jemima's hand then looked at Lena. "Is that okay with you?"

"It's great with me. I know Jemima would love to play."

Beth frowned. "Grandma said you're not Jemima's mother. So who are you?"

Lena considered this. Who was she? "Just a friend," she said.

"A really, really good friend," Jemima proclaimed. Then she turned to Beth. "Where's your mother?"

Beth sighed. "My mother's in heaven."

Jemima's eyes got really wide. "In heaven?"

Beth smiled and took Jemima's hand. "But it's okay. I know she's happy there."

The two had barely left the room when Moira's son came in. "Would you like something to drink?" he asked her in a polite but formal voice. "Coffee, tea, ice water?"

"No thank you," she answered. The truth was she would have loved a cup of coffee. But something about his attitude made her refuse it.

"Okay." He rested his hands on the back of the club chair, just standing there and studying her. Once again she was painfully aware of her less than fashionable ensemble, but she resisted the urge to check for sweater balls on her elbows.

"My mother told me about you." His eyes, like his daughter's, were dark brown. But unlike Beth's, his seemed hard and penetrating. And suddenly she felt as if she were on the witness stand about to be cross-examined by the prosecutor.

"What did she tell you?"

"She mentioned that you were just released from prison."

Lena clasped her hands together and looked directly at him. "That's true."

"And for some reason my mother thinks there's more to your story, or perhaps you got a bum rap or were treated unfairly . . . something to that effect."

Lena didn't respond, but her eyes remained fixed on him. What was he trying to accomplish here? What was his angle? She knew he had one.

"And perhaps my mother is right . . . or maybe not. But I want to make it crystal clear to you that my mother means the world to me, and if anyone tried to take unfair advantage of her kindness and generosity, I wouldn't hesitate to step in." He glanced over his shoulder as if to make sure Moira wasn't nearby. "And it wouldn't be the first time either."

"I see." Lena felt a tightness in her chest and had a sudden urge to jump up and run. Really, what was she doing here?

His features softened slightly. "Just so you know, I'm all for helping people—I mean people who want to be helped and rehabilitated. But not for someone who is only looking for a free ride."

"Well, your mother did offer me the free ride to church. But maybe I shouldn't have accepted."

He smiled as if she'd made a joke. "Well, that's not the kind of free ride I was talking about."

Lena stood. "Perhaps it would be best if Jemima and I left."

"No, no," he said quickly. "Don't do that."

Lena straightened her shoulders and looked him directly in the eyes with a kind of resolve that felt foreign to her. For some reason she wanted to stand up for herself. Maybe she was just sick and tired of being walked on.

"I refuse to stay where I'm not wanted," she began in a firm voice. "You see, Mr. Phillips, I've been through enough false accusations and wrong judgments to last a lifetime. And if I'm about to be subjected to more, I will leave. Please give your mother my apologies."

She looped the handle of her handbag over her arm, picked up her ratty-looking purple parka, and headed off to find Jemima. Enough was enough!

Lena didn't get far. She wasn't even halfway down the stairs before Moira's son had his hand on her shoulder, apologizing like an errant schoolboy. "I'm sorry," he said a bit breathlessly. "It's just that I'm the only one my mother has to watch out for her, and sometimes she needs my protection."

"I understand." She glared at him. "Now if you'll let me go, I'd like to get Jemima and—"

"Please, don't go," he pleaded. "My mother will be so hurt. And then I'll have to tell her it was my fault and—"

"Well, it is your fault, isn't it?"

He rubbed his hand through his short hair. Although it was graying, it appeared to have once been dark like his daughter's. "Yes. I've already said that, and I'm sorry."

"I accept your apology. But I don't care to stay where I'm not welcome."

"Lena?" Moira called from the living room.

"Please," he said quietly. "Just stay for dinner. I don't care whether you forgive my rudeness or not. In fact, you can completely ignore me. But for my mother's sake, stay."

"I don't think—"

"I'll even make it easy for you. I'll leave and you won't

have to put up with me. I'll pretend to have an emergency with a client."

Lena didn't know what to say.

"Lena? Beth? Jemima? Samuel?" Moira called. "Where has everyone gone?"

"I'm coming, Mom." Sam moved past Lena with a hopeful expression. "I'm sorry, Lena. Really, I am. Sometimes I'm just a big buffoon."

Lena followed him up the stairs, keeping a safe distance. She had no idea how to handle this. Everything in her was screaming, *Just leave!* And yet there was Jemima. What would she tell her? And how would she explain this to dear Moira?

"There you are," Moira said as Lena came into the living room.

"The girls went downstairs," Lena said. "I was going to check on them."

"And I got a call from a client who needs my immediate attention," Sam said quickly. "Sorry, Mom, but I'll have to split."

"But it's Sunday—why do you have to work on Sunday?"

"You know what they say . . . no rest for the wicked." He grabbed up his coat and gave her a peck on the cheek.

"Dinner won't be for an hour or so," she called as he was leaving. "Perhaps you'll be done in time to join us."

"I don't know, Mom. I'll come back as soon as I can. If I don't make it, just save me some leftovers." And then he was gone.

Lena felt a mixture of relief and guilt. But Moira seemed perfectly composed as she took Lena's purse and parka and set them on a bench near the foyer. Then she went back to the living room and sat on the sofa, patting the spot beside her. "Come sit with me, Lena."

Lena complied.

"I'm glad the girls are downstairs," Moira told her. "And I'm even glad that my son flew the coop." She chuckled. "I suspect he felt outnumbered by females anyway. Now you and I can really talk."

"Talk?"

"Yes, dear. If you don't mind, I'd like to hear your whole story. And I promise that you can trust me with it. I already know that you've been in prison. But I have a strong impression that it wasn't your fault. Please, tell me what happened. Like I said, the roast won't be ready for another hour anyway."

Lena took in a slow breath. Her story. Would she even be able to tell it? The last time she'd attempted to, no one believed her anyway. Not anyone in the church. Not even her own parents. So she'd simply shut up . . . or maybe she'd shut down.

"I don't even know where to begin, Moira."

"I know your ex-husband was a minister," Moira said, "but not a very good one. Why don't you start there?"

"I'm not sure I can tell everything . . . It's a very painful story."

Moira patted Lena's knee. "But sometimes it's good to tell someone. It might help the wound to heal a bit."

Lena took a deep breath, trying to think of a place to start, something that might help make sense of something so senseless. "My family was always very involved in our church," she began. "My father's grandfather had helped build the church during the Great Depression. Ever since he was a boy, my father had wanted to be a minister. Unfortunately, he wasn't very good at it."

Moira nodded. "Preaching does seem to be a calling, a gift—not everyone would have it."

"Yes, and it frustrated him a lot. It also frustrated him that

I didn't take missions courses in Bible college like he wanted me too. Instead, I took accounting because I loved numbers. After graduation, I worked for a small accounting firm in our town. It wasn't long before my father volunteered me to help with the church's books too. It was only a part-time thing—I did their quarterlies. It was pretty simple and straightforward and I didn't even mind helping."

"Did that make your father happy?"

"I don't know. He never was a happy sort of person. And it bothered him that I didn't get married. He thought that was what all women should do. But I was very shy and I never really dated. In fact, everyone who knew me thought I'd end up an old maid."

"But you're smart and pretty and nice." Moira smiled warmly.

Lena shook her head. "I never felt that way. And when I hit thirty and was still single, I thought I really was going to be a spinster. I lived at home, paying a bit for rent, but also saving my money because I wanted to move out. Naturally, my father was opposed to this. But then he was opposed to almost everything I wanted."

"He sounds like a hard man."

"He was a very hard man." Lena sighed. "Then the minister of our church was retiring, and my dad, being a deacon, brought one of the candidates home for dinner one night. Daniel Markham was being considered for the new minister. And I suspect since he was single, my dad thought he'd make a good husband."

"Oh." Moira nodded. "I get the picture."

"Daniel told us his wife had died a few years ago and that he needed a fresh start. He actually seemed like a nice person. He spoke well. He was nice looking. And although he was almost ten years older than me, I actually felt attracted

71

to him." Lena shuddered to remember those old feelings. It almost made her feel sick to recall that part of her life. How could she have been so deceived?

"So Daniel Markham was selected to replace your minister?" Moira continued for her.

"Yes. And my father's attempt at matchmaking worked. Daniel proposed. Everyone in the church thought it was wonderful. And I even believed I was in love and that Daniel loved me." Lena laughed humorlessly. "But then the marriage began and I realized that instead of escaping my father, which had been my goal, I had married someone just like him. Daniel wouldn't allow me to work outside of the home. I couldn't do anything without getting his approval first. I volunteered at church and continued doing their quarterly financial reports, but Daniel oversaw them."

"Was that how it happened then?" Moira pressed. "The financial reports?"

Lena nodded. "Our church had a strong commitment to missions, and giving was always generous. We'd done lots of fund-raising, and yet over time there seemed to be less money in the mission fund, as well as other places. But when I mentioned this to Daniel, he brushed it off, saying not to worry and that he'd handle it. Or he'd say it was simply a mistake, although I didn't see how. Or he'd make some other excuse or explanation or distract me with a church project. I never questioned him personally about the money. He was the head of the church, the head of our home. My place wasn't to question him. But after a couple of years, the mission board figured out that a very large sum of money was missing." Lena felt a lump in her throat. She vividly remembered the grim faces of the board members, their hostile accusations, and their certainty that she was guilty.

"And you were blamed for it," Moira said softly.

Lena picked a ball of fuzz from the elbow of her sweater. "I was arrested in my home, handcuffed in the kitchen while I was cooking dinner. Embezzlement charges were pressed. At the time, Daniel acted shocked and outraged. He convinced me that he was going to fight it for me. But two days went by and he refused to pay my bail. He said it would be Christlike for me to suffer and that the church would feel compassion, that they would respect me for not fighting back. So I stayed in jail. But no one, including my parents, would even speak to me."

"Oh my." Moira shook her head. "Not even your mother?"

"She was under my father's thumb. I suspect that's what killed her. They both died while I was in prison. The shame, the grief, the stress . . . I'm sure it got to them."

"So they never knew the truth? That you weren't guilty?"

"I tried to tell them the truth. But they believed Daniel over me. In my father's eyes, I'd always been rebellious. I'm sure he thought I was capable of something like that. And Daniel's story made sense to them—he said I stole the money because I wanted to buy a house. Everyone knew I'd wanted to buy a house. But not like that. I had my own money—an inheritance from my grandmother."

"Daniel sounds like an evil man."

"Evil, but conniving and believable and charismatic too. The truth is I even believed him at first. He talked me into staying in jail. He kept up the act that the whole thing was a mistake, but he convinced me that God was at work, that there were lessons for all of us to learn. And he assured me that he'd fix everything and that everyone would apologize to me in time. Of course, his story kept changing. I mean the story he told me. He was stringing me along while he won over everyone on the outside, giving them little clues that hinted at my guilt, building his case."

"What an awful man!"

"Finally Daniel told me that he'd figured the whole thing out. That he'd discovered someone on the mission board had stolen the money. And he planned to catch them but needed to set a trap first. So he talked me into signing over my inheritance—he said he'd use it to bait the trap. He even said the police were in on it. He promised me that I'd be released from jail by the end of the week. He also said it would look good to the church that I donated that much money for missions. And I willingly agreed to his scheme."

"So he took your money too? As well as the church money?"

"Yes. I was such a fool. The whole time I was in jail, Daniel had been setting me up to go down. He'd been lying to everyone and then he lied in court. He stood and made this valiant statement about how he'd been trying to protect me and how he'd realized he'd been wrong to do so, and that he could protect me no longer. He said the truth needed to be told that I was the guilty one and he'd been trying to cover for me. And when I was convicted and sentenced, I just gave up. With so much hurt and humiliation, prison actually sounded better than going back home. It felt like an escape. Well, until I got there. But by then I felt dead inside anyway. Nothing mattered."

"You poor thing." Moira put an arm around Lena's shoulders, pulling her close. "I knew you had a story."

"It's a very ugly story."

"But you knew you were innocent. Didn't you ever consider asking for an appeal or retrial or something?"

"Like I said, I gave up. I was too broken . . . too hurt. I had no fight in me." There was more that Lena could tell, more reasons she chose to give up. But she'd said more than enough for now.

"And that's why you didn't want to go home when you got out of prison."

Lena nodded. "I don't really have a home anymore. A fresh start sounded better. But I'm finding it's harder than I expected."

"At least you have friends." Moira gave her hand a squeeze.

Lena wished that were true. She hoped she had friends. But after Sam's little scene, she wasn't so sure. Although Moira was able to see past her prison record, how would other people feel if they knew she was an ex-con? Maybe there was no such thing as second chances.

CHAPTER
8

After a delicious dinner of roast beef and all the trimmings, Jemima begged to go back down to play Barbies again, and Beth seemed more than willing to join her. "Don't tell any of my friends," she said a bit sheepishly, "but it's kind of fun seeing all the old Barbie outfits and shoes and purses and things. I forgot Barbie had so much cool stuff."

"You should see it, Lena," Jemima said. "She's even got a house and a car and a boat and everything."

Lena laughed as she started to help clear the table. "I think I'm feeling jealous of Barbie."

"No, no," Gretchen told Lena with a severe German accent. "You put dat down. Dis is my job."

Moira nodded. "Don't get in Gretchen's way or you'll be sorry, Lena."

"Das right." Gretchen took the plate from Lena. "I may be old, but I do my job without help, *danke!*"

Lena smiled at her. "Well, thank you, Gretchen. And thank you for the lovely dinner. It's the best meal I've had in years."

Gretchen looked skeptical. "In years?"

"She's telling the truth," Moira said as she took Lena's arm. "Now come with me, I have an idea."

Lena didn't resist as Moira led her through the house, down a hallway, and finally into a large and luxurious bedroom. "What a beautiful room," Lena said as she looked around her. Sky-blue-and-white-striped wallpaper, thick white carpeting, dark wood furnishings, even a marble-faced fireplace.

"Thank you," Moira said. "This is my room. But the reason I brought you back here was because of Barbie."

Lena blinked. "Barbie?"

Moira smiled and pointed at Lena. "I noticed those are the same clothes that you wore on the bus. And I suspect it's all you have since you didn't have any luggage."

Lena nodded.

"Now, I realize I'm an old lady and we're not exactly the same size, but I thought perhaps I might have something you could use."

"Oh, no, Moira," Lena said. "I couldn't possibly take—"

"No, I want to share some things with you." Moira opened up a walk-in closet and turned on the light. "What size are your feet? They look about the same as mine."

Lena looked down at the worn black pumps. "About an eight."

Moira laughed. "I knew it."

"Really, Moira, that's a very kind offer. But I have to say no. You can't give me anything. I insist." Lena felt tears in her eyes. Sometimes it seemed easier to be subjected to cruelty than kindness. It didn't require so much.

"Harrington's isn't the epitome of fashion," Moira called from inside the closet, "but I hardly think you can show up to work wearing the same black pants and red sweater every day, dear. Besides, I really need to thin things out in here. I'm a bit of a clotheshorse, and after Howard died, with full use of the closet, I somehow managed to fill it up."

When Moira emerged with an armful of garments and

wooden hangers clacking together, Lena couldn't hold back any longer. Tears began to flood down her cheeks and she wanted to escape. "Honestly, I—I can't take anything from you. Really, I can't."

Moira dropped the clothes onto her bed then came over and wrapped her arms around Lena. "Well, yes you can, dear. I *want* you to have these things. Don't you understand? It will make me happy."

"But—but . . . your son—he—he won't like it."

Moira held Lena at arm's length, narrowing her eyes with suspicion. "What did Sam say to you anyway?"

"Nothing. But I just can't take—"

"Sit down right there." Moira pointed to a pale blue chair as she picked up a tissue box from her bedside table and held it out to Lena.

Lena pulled out a couple of tissues then sat down and wiped her wet cheeks and blew her nose. How embarrassing.

"Now, tell me, Lena. What exactly did my son say to you?"

"He was only trying to protect you. He didn't want me to take advantage of you. And I don't want to take advantage of you either. I really should go." Lena stood and folded her arms. "You're kind and generous and I treasure your friendship more than you can know. But I cannot take *anything* from you."

"Well, the fact of the matter is you can't go home until I take you home." Moira smiled in a sly sort of way. "And I won't take you home unless you agree to take some of these old clothes off my hands. Good grief, Sam should be thrilled that I'm getting rid of a few things. He knows what a pack rat I am."

"But Moira, I can't."

"Fine, this is what you'll do then. Go and fetch Gretchen for me. Tell her I need help with something. Then you go check on the girls and the Barbies. And I will handle this myself. If Sam ever finds out, which seems hardly likely, you can honestly say you had nothing to do with it." Moira shook her head. "Good grief. He's a good boy, but far too distrustful sometimes. He got that from his father, I'm afraid."

"But I—"

"No buts." Moira shook a wrinkly finger at Lena. "Please, now, do as I say."

Lena blinked then turned and went in search of Gretchen, who was cleaning up in the kitchen. She relayed Moira's message and went downstairs to where Beth and Jemima had created Barbie world. With houses, furnishings, a convertible, clothes galore, horses . . . and all sorts of things that Lena probably would've loved when she was a girl, except her parents said Barbie was wicked.

"Wow." She sat down on the floor next to Jemima and picked up a discarded silver handbag, hanging it on her pinkie finger. "This is really something."

"I know." Jemima beamed at her. "And Beth gave me my very own Barbie and some clothes to take home with me too."

Lena was about to object to this generosity, but she worried that she'd not only get lectured from Moira again but probably hurt Beth as well. Not to mention it would break Jemima's heart. "That's very sweet of you, Beth. I know Jemima didn't have a chance to bring many toys with her when they moved here."

"She told me about that." Beth spoke quietly with a curious expression.

"I didn't tell her everything," Jemima said defensively. "And she promised not to tell anyone."

"That's right. You have my word." Beth held up her hand

like a pledge. "And Jemima said her mom got a job and that's why you're babysitting her."

"Not babysitting," Jemima corrected.

"Right." Beth grinned. "Anyway, Jemima said you were going to work at Harrington's next week and that she might have to take care of herself."

"Oh, I don't think you'll have to take care of yourself," Lena assured Jemima, although she wondered if that's what Sally had told her.

"Anyway, I told her if school was out, I would babysit her. But we still have a couple weeks until Christmas vacation. And then I got this idea."

"Yeah, it's a good idea too," Jemima piped up.

"My high school has a daycare center," Beth told Lena. "I have a child development class where I get to help out in there and it's really fun. But some of the moms got laid off work recently and there aren't too many kids there now, and I'll bet Jemima could stay there when you and her mom have to work."

"That would be fantastic, Beth. I'll be sure to tell Jemima's mom."

"Yeah, she can call New Haven High and ask for Mrs. Price."

Lena made a mental note of this. "Speaking of your mom," she said to Jemima, "she'll be getting off work in about an hour, and you should probably help put the Barbie things away so we can get home before your mom gets there and wonders what happened to us."

Jemima looked disappointed, but she began picking up.

"Come upstairs when you're done," Lena said as she stood. Most of all, she wanted to be out of the house before Sam returned. She couldn't bear the humiliation of having him witness his mother giving her anything. Not even old clothes. She

Melody Carlson

could just imagine the told-you-so expression in his eyes. As if she really had some deep dark plot to swindle his mother.

Fortunately, they got loaded in the car and were on their way back to the boardinghouse without seeing him. In the backseat Jemima clutched a Barbie carrying case to her chest. It contained not just one but two Barbies and a bunch of clothes. Judging by her expression, one might think she'd won the lottery.

"Moira, I don't even know how to thank you," Lena said as they got out of the car and Moira opened the trunk to reveal several grocery bags of clothes.

"I should thank you for helping me clean out my closet."

"No, really, your generosity is overwhelming." Lena's arms were loaded with bags. "Thank you for taking us to church, for dinner, for listening . . . for everything."

"The best thanks you can give me will be to make a success of your fresh start." Moira waved as she opened her car door. "Good luck at Harrington's tomorrow. I'll be sure to come by the store later this week to see how you're doing."

Lena hurried Jemima up the stairs to the boardinghouse. "It's so cold out," she said as she unlocked the front door. "I wonder if it might snow."

"Snow?" Jemima said as they went inside.

"Nah," TJ said as he met them in the doorway with his pack of Camels in hand. "It ain't gonna snow. But there could be an ice storm." He looked at Lena. "You been doing some Christmas shopping?"

"Something like that," she told him as they headed for the stairs. Lena was nearly out of breath when she dropped the heavy bags in her room, and she was just unlocking the door to room 11 when Sally emerged from the stairs as well. Her feet were dragging, but she looked happy to see her daughter.

"Mommy, look!" Jemima held up the pink Barbie carry-all case. "My friend Beth gave me this!"

"Who's Beth?" Sally asked Lena as she bent down to examine Jemima's prize.

Lena quickly explained then told her about the daycare at the high school. "It's New Haven High," she said, "and you can ask for Mrs. Price."

Sally frowned as she went into her room. "But what if they ask questions? What if they want records from her old school?"

"I guess you'll have to figure all that out eventually anyway." Lena stood by the open door.

Sally's brow creased with uncertainty. "I don't know . . ."

"When I'm working, I can't watch Jemima for you," Lena added. "One way or another, you've got to figure out some other form of childcare. Maybe you should enroll her back into school?"

Sally sighed. "Maybe you're right. At least I don't work tomorrow. Not until six anyway. That'll give me a chance to check things out." She dug in her pocket, fishing out several one-dollar bills. "Here. I know it's not much, but—"

"You don't have to pay—"

"What's this?" Sally pointed to the goldfish bowl on the dresser.

"That's Sunshine!" Jemima peered into the bowl. "My very own goldfish."

Lena, not eager to hear how Sally liked Jemima's new pet, stepped into the hallway, wiggled her fingers in a quick goodbye wave, and made a hasty exit.

Back in her room, she kicked off the worn black pumps, cleared a spot on her bed, which was buried in bags, and sat down. What she really wanted was a nap, but Moira's words were still ringing in her ears—the best thanks she could give her kind friend was to make a successful fresh start. That would mean getting a job at Harrington's tomorrow. And to get a job at a nice department store, one needed to look respectable.

She reached for the bag closest to her, pulling out a small stack of neatly folded tops. The first was a basic white cotton shirt with a button-down collar, then a light blue silky blouse with pearly buttons, a pink blouse with decorative stitching, and finally another white blouse that had ruffles and lace like something Lena's grandmother might've worn.

Next she pulled out two cardigans, which, upon a closer look, she realized were both cashmere! One charcoal and one navy. Then she found a black woolen skirt, a pair of navy gabardine trousers, and a charcoal tweed skirt. All three of these garments were fully lined and looked warm. Whether or not they would fit remained to be seen, but they were definitely nice.

Admittedly nothing in this bag screamed high fashion—not that Lena had ever been much into that—but all the garments were in perfect condition and classic in style. And they bore labels with impressive names like Pendleton, Ralph Lauren, and Liz Claiborne, so she knew they hadn't come cheap.

Another bag had shoes. A pair of barely worn brown loafers, ankle-height black leather boots with sensible rubber soles, and finally gorgeous scarlet pumps still in their box. Lena held the pumps up and stared at them in wonder. The soles were perfect, like they'd never been worn, and the heels were stacked and not too high. She set them on the bedside table and opened another bag to find that it contained a couple of nightgowns—the kind that are silky on the outside but flannel on the inside—and several pairs of what looked like never-worn granny panties. She held up a pair and giggled. At least this was better than washing her one pair out each night and hanging it over the heat register to dry. There were also a couple packages of panty hose, a pair of slippers, some trouser socks, several pretty silk scarves, a pair of brown leather gloves, and some simple but nice costume jewelry.

Lena continued to lay things out on her bed, arranging tops with skirts or pants, adding a scarf here or a necklace there. She marveled at the selections Moira and Gretchen had made. As if they were both professional wardrobe planners. Or perhaps just angels in disguise.

Finally she came to the last and biggest bag, a shopping bag from Harrington's. On the top was a neatly folded plaid woolen scarf, and beneath it was a red woolen coat trimmed with white fur. This was the very coat that Moira had worn on the bus when they met the other day—the Santa coat! Lena laughed to remember how Moira hadn't cared for the coat and how she'd explained it was from her sister. Of course she was eager to get rid of it.

Lena lifted the coat up and slipped it on. The heavy satin lining felt luxurious, and she could tell the coat would be much warmer than her purple parka. She was curious as to how it looked on her, but the only mirror in her room was a small wall mirror. She peered into it and realized that if she wanted to get a job tomorrow, she might need to do something about her hair and perhaps add a bit of color to her face. Her father had never approved of makeup, but Lena had always felt better with a bit of blush and lip color.

She had noticed a drug store on Main Street and now wondered if it might possibly be open. She grabbed her purse and parka and decided to find out. The wind was icy cold as she hurried along, trying to calculate in her head just how much, or how little, she would allow herself to spend. Although it was an investment in her future.

The drugstore felt warm and friendly, but she knew she

didn't have time to dawdle, since according to the sign on the door and the clock inside, they would be closing in about twenty minutes.

"Can I help you?" a woman in a white jacket asked.

"Oh, I'm just looking for some bargains," Lena said. "You see, I arrived in town without a few things, like lipstick and blush, but I don't want to spend much."

The woman pointed to a nearby table. "Everything there is marked down with an additional fifty percent off."

Lena moved to the cluttered table. It seemed to have a bit of everything on it. Before long she found a rosy-colored lip and blush compact for only $1.80, as well as a package of opened sponge rollers—with two rollers missing—for less than a dollar. And a small bottle of lavender lotion for a dollar as well. On her way to the cash register she noticed packages of plastic hangers for a dollar and decided her lovely new clothes deserved to be hung up properly. She fished out five dollars from the tip money Sally had given her and was pleased to get back a bit of change. Then she hurried back to Miller House and up to her room to put things away.

She knew her hair really needed a good cut, but that would have to come later—after she got her first paycheck. For now, she would wash it and dry it over the heating vent then roll it on the green sponge rollers and hope for the best. Her plan was to show up at Harrington's when they opened at nine tomorrow. She would do everything possible to put her best foot forward.

If she had a bit more faith or some kind of assurance that God still cared about her—and she felt bad that she didn't— she would've prayed before going to sleep. As it was, she was encouraged that she was slightly hopeful for her future. That in itself was just short of miraculous.

CHAPTER
9

Once again Lena woke before the sun. Thanks to the sponge rollers, she hadn't had a particularly restful night. But that didn't matter as she slipped into the bathroom to take a shower. As usual, the bathroom was less than tidy, so she gave the shower stall a quick cleanup before and after, again leaving it cleaner than she had found it. Now if only the other tenants would do likewise.

Her stomach rumbled as she dressed. She'd decided on the tweed skirt, the white shirt topped with the charcoal cardigan, and the red and black paisley scarf for an accent. It had looked attractive laid out on her bed. How it looked on her was a mystery. But at least the clothing fit—mostly. The waist of the skirt was a bit large, but she used a black leather belt to cinch it in a bit and covered it with the cardigan, hoping no one would notice.

What to wear on her feet was a challenge. Her old worn black pumps probably matched best except they looked cheap. If the black boots had been taller, they would've been perfect. The loafers looked too casual. And the red shoes, while very pretty, seemed a bit over the top. Still, she wanted to make an impression, so it would be the red shoes. She would just wear the boots to walk to the store and switch them out for the shoes in the restroom.

Next she removed the foam curlers from her hair. To her surprise, her hair was curlier than ever before. When she looked in the mirror, instead of her straight, shoulder-length sandy hair, her curls resembled those of Shirley Temple, which caused her round face to look even rounder. Perhaps the cold weather would straighten it out a bit as she walked to the store. Anyway, it was probably an improvement.

She applied a bit of lip color and blush, and although she wouldn't call herself attractive, she looked a little healthier and possibly like someone who could work in a department store. At least she hoped so.

She pulled up the shade and peered out the window. Judging by the light outside, she suspected it was getting close to nine. And since it looked frosty and cold out, she decided to wear the Santa coat, which would certainly look better than that horrid purple parka with the broken zipper.

With her red pumps in her purse, she began her trek toward Main Street. The town was fairly quiet and the sidewalks a bit slippery, so she was careful to watch her step. Pausing by the drugstore, she saw that it was already open, so it must be after nine by now.

With a fluttering in her stomach—either nerves or hunger—she pushed open a heavy glass door and entered Harrington's. She was met with warmth and Christmas music, and a tall tree decked out in silver and gold towered in the foyer. Everywhere she looked, the store was perfection. While the racks and shelves didn't seem overly stocked, there appeared to be plenty of merchandise to choose from.

"May I help you?" asked a young woman in the accessories department.

"I'm just looking," Lena said with a forced smile. Really,

it wasn't untrue. She was looking. She continued walking through the store, perusing the various departments until she came to the escalator and read the directory posted there. Both the restroom and the main office were located on the third floor, so she went up.

She made a quick shoe change in the restroom, which was impressively clean. She considered removing her coat and folding it over her arm, but it was rather bulky and seemed easier to simply wear until she found a place to hang it up. She checked her image in the mirror and almost didn't recognize herself.

Holding her head high, she approached the office area.

"May I help you?" asked an older woman behind the counter.

"I'm here to see about a job." Lena recited her carefully rehearsed line.

"I'm sorry, we're not taking applications right now." The woman gave her a sympathetic smile.

"But I was told that—"

"It doesn't really matter what you were told, Harrington's is not hiring."

"But I was promised a job."

"We've had to lay off employees." The woman's voice grew firmer. "Trust me, there are no jobs available."

"But a friend set this up," she persisted. "A Mrs. Stanfield. I believe she's a friend of Mrs. Harrington's."

"That makes no difference." The woman shook her head. "We are not hiring. Now if you'll excuse me."

Lena just stood there, watching as the woman picked up the phone. Hopefully she wasn't calling security. Even so, Lena wasn't ready to give up. Perhaps she should've asked for an appointment with Mrs. Harrington. A chance to explain her situation and plead for a job. Even a job with partial pay.

"Hurry up," a woman's voice said from behind her.

"I'm coming, Mom," a younger voice said.

Lena turned to see a tall woman emerging from what seemed to be a private office. Her auburn hair was cut to perfection, and she wore a stylish, camel-colored suit with the jacket cinched in by a brown leather belt that matched her handbag and tall brown boots.

"Come on, Cassidy, we're going to be late for your appointment. Hurry, sweetheart."

A preteen girl came out. She was dressed more casually in khaki pants and a jean jacket. Her hair, the same color as the woman's, was long and thick. It seemed obvious they were mother and daughter. But to Lena's surprise, the girl stopped in her tracks when she saw her. She looked at Lena with large green eyes. "Who are you?" she asked.

Lena smiled. "I'm Lena Markham. Who are you?"

The girl smiled back. "Cassidy."

"Come on, Cassidy." Her mother was by the restrooms, looking a little flustered. "We need to go *now*."

"Just a minute, Mom." Cassidy turned back to Lena. "Why are you here?"

"I, uh, I was looking for a job."

Cassidy's eyes lit up. "Mom, she's looking for a job," she called out.

"Cassidy." The mother's voice sounded impatient.

"But, Mom."

"We don't have time for this."

"But you have to talk to her, Mom." Cassidy looked back at Lena then lowered her voice. "Come back here at 3:00, okay?"

Uncertain, Lena looked from Cassidy to her mother.

"I mean it," the girl called as she hurried to join her mom. And just like that, they were gone. Lena noticed the woman behind the counter was staring at her.

"What just happened?" Lena asked her.

The woman shook her head. "I'm not sure."

"The girl told me her name was Cassidy, but who is she?"

"Cassidy Harrington."

Lena slowly nodded. "So that was Mrs. Harrington with her?"

"*Ms.* Harrington. She divorced her husband and went back to her maiden name."

"Oh. Did you hear what Cassidy said to me? About being here at three?"

The woman chuckled. "I did, but I can't imagine why."

"Should I come?"

She shrugged. "That's up to you."

❦

Despite the cold temperatures and freezing rain, Lena came back to Harrington's a bit before three. She had a feeling she was on a fool's errand, but her curiosity—and desperation—forced her to return. She was coming up the escalator when she heard a voice call out, "There she is, Mom. I told you she'd come back."

Lena stepped off the elevator and smiled at the mother and daughter. "I'm not sure why I came back, because I heard you're not hiring. But I was compelled."

"I'm Ms. Harrington," the woman told her in a slightly irritated voice.

"I'm Lena Markham and my friend Mrs. Stanfield told me—"

"You seem to have met my daughter Cassidy already. And she is insistent that that I give you an interview, Ms. Markham."

Cassidy winked at Lena.

"Thank you," Lena told Ms. Harrington. "I really do appreciate you taking the—"

"Right this way, please." Ms. Harrington smiled at her daughter. "And you will kindly wait in the employees' lounge for me. And start your homework. And make sure you have one of those protein drinks and *not* soda."

Cassidy nodded, watching as her mother led Lena into her office.

"Please, have a seat." Ms. Harrington gestured to a pair of black leather chairs across from her desk. "I'll cut to the chase because I'm sure your time is as valuable as mine."

Lena wasn't so sure, but she nodded then sat down, folding her hands in her lap.

"Cassidy seems to think that you've been sent here by angels or God or maybe even Santa Claus."

Lena blinked. "What?"

"She thinks you'd be perfect to play Mrs. Santa."

"Mrs. Santa?"

"I suppose it's that coat." Ms. Harrington frowned. "And the curly hair. And I guess you have the right sort of face too." Now she laughed. "But I'm also guessing that is not the sort of work you're looking for."

Lena was too dumbfounded to respond.

"Yes, I'm not surprised. It's what I told Cassidy would happen—that you'd be insulted. Please accept my apologies. Unfortunately, I'm fully aware that most Santa jobs usually go to drunks and degenerates. In fact, that's why we lost our last Santa."

"And that was a woman?" Lena ventured. "Mrs. Santa?"

Ms. Harrington waved her hand. "No, no, we've never even had a Mrs. Santa. That was totally Cassidy's idea. I don't even know where she came up with it or why. But not only was her heart set on finding the perfect Mrs. Santa, she's equally determined to play Mrs. Santa's helper as an elf this year." She sighed in a tired way. "Not that I'm encouraging her to do that."

"I see." Lena wasn't sure what to do. Of course she had no desire to play Mrs. Santa, and yes, it was somewhat insulting. Did this mean Ms. Harrington thought that Lena was a drunk or degenerate too? Not that she'd expected to be hired as a bookkeeper or anything too impressive. But Mrs. Santa?

And yet, who was she to be choosy? She was desperate for a job. Even if it was only temporary.

"But you're right, Ms. Markham, we're not hiring. In fact, I've just had to lay off several employees. And that wasn't easy to do right before Christmas." She sighed. "I'm afraid this will be the last Christmas for Harrington's."

"I'm sorry."

"So I won't waste any more of your time." She stood and smiled stiffly.

Lena stood too. "But what if I wanted to play Mrs. Santa?"

Ms. Harrington blinked. "Are you serious?"

Lena gave a nervous smile. "I actually am in need of a job."

Ms. Harrington looked relieved. "Then you've got one."

"Do you want me to fill out an—"

"Talk to Dorothy in the office. She'll give you some papers and things to sign, and then go down to alterations and talk to Brynn. She's already started making a costume and she'll want to do a fitting."

Lena's thoughts were racing. Was this a mistake? Should she mention her prison record? Or did it even matter, considering the way Ms. Harrington had described Santa employees as drunks and degenerates? Especially since Lena was neither.

"Hurry now," she told Lena. "Dorothy will give you your

schedule. If the costume is ready, I see no reason you can't begin tomorrow."

By the end of the day, Lena had filled out the proper paperwork and had been fitted in what was actually a rather attractive red velvet dress trimmed with white fur, not unlike her Santa coat. She also had a white, lace-trimmed apron, a little cap, and even a pair of granny-style wire-rimmed glasses. Everyone agreed that she should forgo the wig and stick with her own hair, which, although not white, had a grayish look in a dishwater blonde sort of way. "Just make sure you keep it curled like that," Cassidy had told her.

Lena also had a schedule. She was expected to work from noon until eight, with two thirty-minute breaks, every day until Christmas, which meant she'd get some overtime pay. Her hourly pay was only minimum wage and the first payday wasn't until Saturday, but she had already done the math, figuring she would make around $250 a week after taxes. Not much, but plenty for now. What happened after Christmas was anyone's guess.

Lena had also toured the "North Pole" situated in a corner of the basement. She'd even tried out the big Santa chair, which, despite looking plush, was actually rather hard. And Cassidy was getting someone to make adjustments to the various signs—changing them from Santa to Mrs. Santa.

As Lena walked home, she knew she'd have to keep her new job a secret from Jemima since she was still young enough to believe in Santa Claus and might even want to come visit Mrs. Santa at Harrington's. And to keep it from Jemima meant she might as well keep it from everyone in the boardinghouse, since someone with loose lips, like TJ, would probably blow her cover anyway.

"Did you get a job?" Sally asked as they met in the hallway between their rooms while Jemima was using the bathroom.

"I did." Lena smiled.

Sally frowned. "Oh. I know it was selfish, but I was hoping you hadn't."

"Sorry. No luck with childcare?"

"When the daycare lady found out that Jemima was school age, she said she needed to be enrolled."

"But maybe that's for the best. That way Jemima can make friends."

"I explained the situation with my husband and she seemed to understand. She gave me the name of a social worker I'm supposed to meet with tomorrow."

"I can watch Jemima for you tonight," Lena offered. "And any other time before noon or after eight . . . although that's probably not much help."

Sally smiled. "Thanks. And sorry I'm being so glum. Congratulations on the job. Working at Harrington's must be nice."

"It seems like a pleasant store. But I don't get tips."

Sally nodded. "Yeah. Getting tips and free food is a real perk. In fact, why don't you bring Jemima for dinner tonight?" She handed Lena some bills. "My treat."

"Sounds good." The truth was Lena was ravenous and slightly envious that Sally had gotten what seemed the better of the two jobs. Lena thought she'd gladly switch with Sally if she could. Even the hard work of waiting tables seemed preferable to playing Mrs. Santa. Plus there was a lot more job security. Still, a temporary job was better than nothing.

After dining fairly economically on grilled cheese sandwiches and soup and spending every cent that Sally had given her, Lena and Jemima returned to the room to play Barbies and get ready for bed. Once again Jemima begged for Lena to tell her *'Twas the Night Before Christmas*. As Lena said, "A happy Christmas to all, and to all a good-night," she realized she was actually starting to feel like Mrs. Santa. Perhaps it was a good sign.

Of course, later on as she was drifting to sleep in her own bed, wearing the foam curlers again, she wondered, how would bright-eyed, expectant children react to seeing Mrs. Santa rather than Santa Claus himself? What if they were disappointed? Or even cried? How would she handle that?

"Where's Santa?" a scowling preschool-aged boy demanded. If Lena had only had a dollar for each time she'd answered that question, she might be able to retire her fur-trimmed dress by the end of the week. And this was only her first day.

"Where do you think Santa is?" she answered cheerfully.

The boy's brow creased. "Feeding his reindeer?"

"Yes, that and making lots of toys and getting ready for Christmas. You know, someone has to keep track of all those elves at the North Pole. Otherwise they might have a big party and forget all about Christmas. Do you have any idea how naughty elves can be when left to themselves?"

He shook his head.

"Well, they're a lot like little boys and girls. Sometimes they can't help but be naughty." She smiled as she lifted him onto her lap. "Fortunately, Santa understands this. Both about his elves and all the boys and girls. Now, tell me, Tyler, what do you want for Christmas?"

"Hey, how do you know my name?" he asked.

Lena glanced at Cassidy. Her elf assistant, dressed in a green velvet vest and shorts over red tights, would discreetly pen the name of the next child in line on a whiteboard. She would then flash this at Lena as she escorted the child toward the chair. It was a good system.

"Because I'm Mrs. Santa," she told Tyler with a smile.

"I want Legos," Tyler told her with serious eyes. "And I want my daddy to come to my house and help me build a really big spaceship with them."

"Legos are great fun," she said. "And I'm sure your daddy will want to play with them too, but you might have to invite him."

Tyler rattled off a few more things, and as usual, she reminded him that Santa had his limits, but she would do her best to tell him of Tyler's request. Then she handed him a candy cane and said, "Merry Christmas!" just as the photographer snapped a photo.

So it went on into the evening. To her relief and surprise, no toddlers ran screaming from her. And more than one mother mentioned that Mrs. Santa was a lot less intimidating than Mr. Claus himself.

"Someone should've thought of this years ago," a mom said as she peeled her little girl off of Lena's lap. "My son wouldn't go near Santa when he was this age."

"Go, Mrs. Santa. This is one more step for women's lib." Another mother raised her fist and several of the moms laughed.

"I told my mom that Mrs. Santa would be a big hit," Cassidy said. She hung up a sign that read, "Mrs. Santa is on the phone with Santa right now. She'll be back after she helps him make his list and check it twice." Cassidy looked at her watch and set the fake clock to 6:30 p.m., then the two slipped back to their makeshift break room, which consisted of several patio chairs, a round table, a small refrigerator, and a microwave, all tucked behind the set of the North Pole. This private spot was deemed necessary since, as Cassidy pointed out, neither Mr.

nor Mrs. Santa could get very far through the store without drawing a small crowd of little ones. Hardly a break.

"What gave you the Mrs. Santa idea in the first place?" Lena asked as she opened a bottle of water, which was provided by the store for free.

"I actually had a dream one night a few weeks ago. It was so real. I felt like I was at the North Pole and I was talking to Mrs. Santa." Cassidy checked the mirror to see if her pointy green velvet hat was still on right. "In my dream, I asked Mrs. Santa why she never came to visit the kids at the store. I mean I knew that our Santa wasn't the real guy and I know Santa isn't real, but in my dream it seemed so real. Like I was really talking to Mrs. Santa." She turned and looked at Lena. "And she looked just like you."

Lena laughed.

"Seriously, Lena. When I saw you upstairs yesterday, I almost fell over. It was like, there she is—Mrs. Santa." She cocked her head to one side. "You're not really her, are you?"

Lena gave her a mysterious smile. "What do you think?"

Cassidy laughed. "I don't know what I think. But I was praying that Mrs. Santa would show up. And here you are." She looked puzzled. "Really, where did you come from? And how did you know to come to our store?"

"Ah . . ." Lena held a finger to her chin. "I can't tell all my secrets now, can I?"

As Cassidy pestered her for more answers, Lena wondered what she would think if she knew that Lena had come here straight from prison. She felt a stab of guilt for the way she'd answered—or not answered—one of the questions on the employment application. It was about prior felony convictions. Instead of answering yes or no as indicated, she had made a very small asterisk (as in "see below"), and she'd placed another asterisk on the back where she wrote in tiny letters: *Falsely convicted*. It wasn't untrue. But perhaps the way she'd done it was slightly deceitful.

Still, she knew that if she'd checked "yes," the assumption would be that she was a criminal. And she was not. *Worst-case scenario*, she'd told herself as she'd handed Dorothy all the papers, *is that I'll have to explain*. And when no one had asked, she hadn't said anything either. Why should she?

"Are you married?" Cassidy persisted.

"I'm Mrs. Santa," she said, continuing her charade. "Goodness gracious, of course I'm married."

"Do you have any children?"

Lena slowly shook her head. "No . . . no children. I always wanted children though." She smiled. "Of course, there are the elves. They're like my children and I do miss them so."

Cassidy giggled.

Lena winked. "But you make a nice little elf."

"Tell me, Mrs. Santa, where do you live when you're *not* at the North Pole?"

"In a boardinghouse for now," Lena said. "Just a small room with a narrow little bed. But I do miss the sound of Santa's snoring. It's a bit lonely at times."

"You make this so believable."

"And when all the rush of Christmas is over with, Santa and I like to take a couple of weeks down in the Florida Keys. Did you know Santa actually won an Ernest Hemingway look-alike contest last year?"

Cassidy laughed even harder. "Okay, okay, I believe you already."

"Well, it's about time. I was afraid I was going to have to get Santa on the phone for real, and he's so busy just now." Lena glanced at the clock. "Speaking of time, we should probably get back out there."

The children were a bit older this time of night. And a bit

more cynical. One girl who looked to be about seven stuck out her lip and said, "I know Santa Claus isn't real and neither are you."

Lena smiled. "Oh, but I am real." She stuck out her hand. "Here, pinch me and see if it hurts."

The girl pinched her and Lena said, "Ouch! See, that proves I'm real, doesn't it?"

The girl looked slightly confused.

Lena looked over to where the mom was waiting with an older girl. "Tell me, Faith Ann," Lena said quietly. "Did your older sister tell you that Santa wasn't real?"

She nodded with wide eyes. "How did you know?"

Lena laughed. "And does Santa still bring your older sister gifts for Christmas?"

She nodded again.

"Then you should ask your sister where the gifts are coming from and why she keeps saying what she wants Santa to bring her."

Faith Ann's eyes lit up. "Yeah. You're right."

Lena wasn't sure if it was right or wrong, but when they were done talking, it seemed that Faith Ann's faith in Santa had been restored. Really, what did it hurt? Lena knew her father would probably turn over in his grave—or wherever he was—if he knew his daughter, the ex-con, was playing this role. But what was the harm in making children happy? Based on the stories she'd heard today, some of these children (not unlike Jemima) needed a spark of joy in their dreary little lives. And it made her happy to provide them with it. Really, this was a great job!

Lena still felt it was a great job on Friday. Oh, her lap was a bit sore, and she didn't particularly enjoy the teasing she got from fellow employees, but she tried to take it with good humor. It was the children who made her appreciate this job—she loved chatting with the little ones, catching them off guard, and even hearing some of their secrets, both the good and the not so good. And she always tried to give them a bit of hope to take with them. It seemed the least she could do.

Lena was also growing quite fond of her young elf helper, and she looked forward to Cassidy's arrival after school each day. Not that the other elf, Patricia from the children's department, wasn't good. But her sugar-sweet voice got on Lena's nerves at times, and she was always relieved to see the shift change.

"Are you going to work every day?" Lena asked Cassidy during their last break. "Or will you take weekends off?"

Cassidy frowned. "Mom says I have to take weekends off."

Lena nodded. "That makes sense. After all, you're pretty young to be working all these hours."

"That's what Mom says too. She said next week she's cutting me back to just three hours a day."

Lena wasn't surprised about that either. In fact, it seemed a little odd that a twelve-year-old was working this much. Except for the fact that Cassidy did a superb job with the kids. It was obvious they liked her more than Patricia no matter how hard the elder elf tried. Maybe the kids were suspicious of her saccharine voice too.

"Have a good weekend," Lena told Cassidy after they'd changed back into their street clothes at the end of their shift.

"I'll miss you, Mrs. Santa," Cassidy called as she went to join her mother. Ms. Harrington smiled and waved almost as if she appreciated Lena. This small gesture gave Lena a bit of hope—perhaps there would be a job for her beyond Christmas after all. Though it seemed unlikely, since from what she was hearing, sales were down and most of the employees cringed when they saw Ms. Harrington coming around.

※

On Saturday, Lena was surprised to see Moira and Beth standing among the moms and kids. Certainly Beth didn't plan to get her photo taken on Mrs. Santa's lap. Although several teen girls had popped down here thinking that they'd get a picture with Santa, when they saw that it was Lena instead, they'd changed their minds. Something about a teen girl sitting on the lap of a middle-aged woman was a bit off-putting. To Lena as well.

Finally the line dwindled and it was nearly break time, but Moira and Beth were still there. "Are you here to see Mrs. Santa?" Patricia chirped at Beth.

Beth giggled. "Kind of. Can we talk to her?"

"Sure. It's almost break time though."

Moira and Beth came up to her chair, and it was obvious they knew who she was, although she'd been hoping to keep it incognito. "Mrs. Santa," Moira said with a twinkle in her eye. "Do you have a few minutes to chat?"

Lena nodded. "Do you want to come to the back room?"

"We were hoping to take you to lunch," Beth said.

"In this?" Lena held out her arms.

"We didn't know you were Mrs. Santa," Moira confessed. "Until I went up and asked Camilla whether or not you were working here and she set me straight. She seems to really like you, Lena."

"Her daughter works as my elf part-time," Lena said as she led them toward the make-do break room. "The Mrs. Santa thing was actually Cassidy's idea."

"I wish I could be an elf," Beth said longingly. "It looks like fun."

Lena watched as Patricia set the break clock and scurried off. "I wish you could too, Beth."

"If any openings arise, let me know."

Moira frowned as they sat down in the patio chairs. "I'm surprised Camilla would allow Cassidy to work like this."

"Cassidy loves being an elf," Lena told them. "She actually had a dream that she was talking to Mrs. Santa. Working here like this has been a dream come true for her."

"That is so sweet," Beth said. "How is she doing anyway?"

"Cassidy?"

Moira and Beth exchanged glances.

"What?" Lena asked.

"You don't know?" Moira looked concerned.

"Know what?"

"Oh." Moira shook her head. "Cassidy has leukemia. She was in remission last year. But I heard she'd been getting chemo treatments again this past fall."

"Seriously?" Lena gasped. "But she seems healthy to me."

"She's a little trouper," Moira said.

"She's so happy . . . and helpful." Lena tried to imagine the vivacious girl having chemo treatments. It just didn't make sense.

"Perhaps she's doing better now," Moira said. "Whatever the situation, I know Camilla would never let Cassidy work if she thought her health was at risk."

"And maybe Cassidy feels better when she's doing something like this," Beth said. "It might take her mind off things."

"She does seem to enjoy the children." Still, Lena felt sickened by this news. Sweet Cassidy . . . leukemia . . . it seemed so unfair.

"So, how are *you* doing?" Moira asked Lena.

"I'm doing fine." Lena nodded. "It's great to be working. Not exactly what I expected, but I'm having fun."

"And will you and Jemima want a ride to church again on Sunday?"

"That would be nice. Jemima has talked about it. She had fun at Sunday school."

"Then it's a date."

"And I thought maybe I could help babysit Jemima if both you and her mom are working," Beth said.

Lena explained that Sally was working right now and that Jemima was being watched by an elderly woman at the boardinghouse. "It's not the best situation, but Sally is okay with it."

"We'll stop by the café and speak to her," Moira said.

"I want to thank you again for the beautiful clothes." Lena looked down at her red velvet dress. "As it turned out, I didn't even need them. Would you like me to return them?"

"Of course not. They're all yours, dear. I was happy to thin the herd. Goodness, how many things can one clotheshorse wear anyway?"

Beth laughed. "Dad's always saying I'm just like Grandma," she told Lena. "You should see *my* closet!"

They chatted for most of Lena's break, which really did help to pass the time. Then Moira promised she'd see her tomorrow. "Same time, same place," she called as she waved goodbye.

It being Saturday, the store was busier than usual. And the children seemed to just keep coming. But about an hour before closing, Lena noticed a familiar face among the mothers. She looked discreetly her way, trying to remember how she possibly knew her. Was the woman from prison? If so, would she remember Lena and mention it? And if she did, how would Lena react?

The woman, who appeared to be in her twenties, walked up, leading her small son by the hand. Pausing, she peered at Lena curiously and then said, "Lena Markham?"

Lena smiled. "I'm sorry, you must be mistaking me for someone else." She waved to the sign over her chair. "I am Mrs. Santa. And who have we here?"

The woman frowned. "This is Preston." When Lena opened her arms, the little guy toddled right up to her and she pulled him onto her lap, smiling toward the camera since it was mostly about the photos with these little ones.

"Well, Preston, let me guess what you want for Christmas . . . how about a tricycle?"

He seemed happy and clapped his hands. But his mother kept staring.

"Now you be a good little boy and I'll tell Santa to bring you something really special." She smiled at the woman.

"I know that's you, Lena Markham." The woman spoke quietly as she reached over and snatched her son. "You were Pastor Markham's wife. You're the one who stole the missions money from church. I was in high school then and I'd worked hard to raise some of that money." She held her son close to her. "And I can't believe you're here doing this. You should be ashamed of yourself."

"Is something wrong?" Patricia asked as she was escorting a school-aged boy up to the chair.

"Ask her," the woman said with narrowed eyes.

Suddenly Lena remembered. That had to be Justine Grant—all grown up and just about as mean as her mother, Marsha Grant, had been.

"What's wrong with her?" Patricia quietly asked Lena.

"She's a very angry young woman." Lena shook her head then turned to smile down at the boy. "You must be Brian," she said to him. She proceeded to guess correctly about the video game he wanted. It wasn't a hard guess since most of the boys his age had requested the hot new game. But the whole time she made small talk with Brian, she was thinking about Justine, wondering what the young woman might do. Or perhaps she would do nothing. Lena could only hope.

Lena felt bone tired when her workday ended. Whether this exhaustion was from all the children she'd spent time with or a result of worrying over Justine Grant was unclear. But as she put on her street clothes and hurried through the store, all she wanted to do was go home and sleep. And yet she still had to watch Jemima. She had promised to take over for old Mrs. Davies when she got back. But when she went to Mrs. Davies's room on the first floor, she found the old woman had already gone to bed.

"Where's Jemima?" Lena asked.

"That girl took her." Mrs. Davies clutched her robe around her.

"What girl?" Lena demanded.

"I don't know her name. But Sally brought her here and they took her."

"Sally brought her?"

Mrs. Davies nodded. "Now, if you don't mind, I'd like to go back to bed."

"Okay. I'm sorry for disturbing you."

"Oh, yes, I think they're bringing Jemima back for you to watch since Sally is working really late tonight."

"Oh. I better go see."

"Yes, you better."

So instead of going to bed like she wanted, Lena waited in the lobby, and after about fifteen minutes Beth came in with Jemima. And her father was shadowing them. Lena could tell he wasn't sure what to make of the boardinghouse, and he was probably fretting that his daughter was going to get mugged inside. To be fair, she couldn't blame him.

"Thank you for watching Jemima," Lena told Beth.

"I went to Beth's house," Jemima said. "She has a pool table and video games and all kinds of stuff."

Lena nodded then looked at Sam. "Thank you for bringing Jemima back."

He shrugged. "Don't see that I had much choice."

"Oh, Dad," Beth said. "Why are you such a grump?"

He looked slightly embarrassed. "Sorry. It's been a long day."

"For all of us, I'm sure." Lena reached down to take Jemima's hand. "We should get you to bed."

Beth mouthed something to Lena, like she didn't want Jemima to hear. "What?" Lena asked.

"I didn't say anything to her . . . you know, about your job." Beth winked.

"Oh." Lena nodded. "Good for you. Thanks!"

Sam looked curiously at her and Lena could tell he didn't know about her job either. And why should he?

She thanked them both again then herded Jemima up the stairs. "If we don't hurry, we won't have time for a story," she said as they went.

"The Christmas story again?"

"If you want it."

"Yes, yes—the Christmas story!" Jemima ran up the stairs so fast that Lena could barely keep up.

CHAPTER
11

Lena and Jemima went to church with Moira again. But this time Lena couldn't stay for Sunday dinner because of work, and when Beth said she was watching Jemima again, Moira suggested that perhaps Sam could give Lena a ride too. "That way I can meet my girlfriends for lunch," she confessed.

So Lena found herself sitting in the front seat of Sam's silver BMW, with Beth and Jemima in the back. "This is a beautiful car," she said in an effort to make small talk. She wanted to add, *It must've cost a bundle*, but controlled herself.

"Tell her *why* you got this car," Beth called from behind them.

"Why don't *you* tell her?" he said.

"I made him get it," Beth said. "He'd been driving around this ugly-bugly maroon minivan, and I was so embarrassed to be seen with him that I said he had to get a new car. He told me that if he was going to do that, I would have to pick it out."

"That was a mistake," Sam muttered.

"Oh, you love this Beamer, Dad. Admit it."

"I had no problem with the minivan, Beth. I still miss it sometimes."

Beth groaned.

Lena was caught off guard by this story. She had assumed

that Sam was the kind of guy who needed a fancy car to boost his ego. Apparently she'd been wrong.

"So how's the job?" he asked Lena in a gesture she knew was simply politeness. "Beth told me a bit about it. Sounds interesting."

"I'm enjoying it," she said. "It wasn't exactly what I expected, but I couldn't be happier."

"Camilla Harrington is a good friend of mine," he said. "She and Cassidy have been through some tough times."

"Well, Cassidy is a gem," Lena told him. "She helps me during the week, but I really miss her when she's gone."

"Don't forget what I told you, Lena," Beth said. "If they need another elf girl, I'm available."

"Seems you have your hands full with babysitting," her dad reminded her.

"Maybe I can be an elf girl too," Jemima said.

"I think you have to be older," Beth said.

"What is an elf girl anyway?"

"Remember," Lena said, "elves are Santa's helpers. But they live at the North Pole and that would be an awfully long commute for you. Besides, your mommy would miss you."

"Oh."

"What kind of work will you do when this job ends?" Sam asked quietly.

"Whatever kind I can find, I suppose. Although I doubt I'll find anyone who'll give me an accounting job. That's what I was trained for."

"No, I doubt that too."

Fortunately they were nearly there. Lena profusely thanked him for the ride and then thanked Beth for helping with Jemima. She promised Jemima that she'd see her after work. "And we'll have a different story tonight," she said.

"I don't want a different story," Jemima said. "I like the Christmas one."

"We'll find another Christmas one," she said as she opened the car door. "I'm sure a store will have books."

"As long as it's a Christmas story." Jemima nodded. "Then that's okay."

Lena waved, closed the door, and hurried into the store. She loved Moira and Beth, but it was unfortunate they seemed to come as a package deal—with Sam. Not that Sam was a bad person. He was probably okay. But he had a way of making Lena feel nervous and defensive and almost as if she'd really done something to have deserved her eight years in prison. In fact, in some ways he reminded her of her dad.

She hurried toward the escalator, eager to get down to the basement, put on her Mrs. Santa dress, and push thoughts of guilt or prison or worry or unhappiness behind her.

"Lena?"

She turned to see Ms. Harrington standing by the directory sign near the escalator. She smiled, but her lips seemed tight, almost as if something was wrong. "Can I see you in my office before you go to work?"

"Sure." Lena stepped behind her on the escalator. As she studied Ms. Harrington's straight back, garbed in a charcoal gray dress that looked very expensive, Lena felt worried. Something was wrong. Had Justine said something? Phoned in a complaint? Made an accusation? She braced herself as she followed her boss into her office.

"Please, sit." Ms. Harrington waved to a black leather chair and Lena sat.

"Is something wrong?" Lena asked.

She nodded. "It's about Cassidy."

"Cassidy?"

"I wasn't going to tell you about her illness. That's the way she wanted it. But I feel you need to know."

"Actually, I do know. Moira Phillips is a friend of mine and she mentioned it yesterday. But I had no idea before she said anything."

"Oh, well, that's good. I felt you should know. And although she's been doing better, she has her spells . . . Today she's not so well."

"I'm so sorry." Lena felt her eyes filling. She knew it was partly due to her worry that Justine had blown her cover, but it was mostly out of concern for Cassidy. "She is such a sweet girl. I love working with her."

"That's just it." Ms. Harrington clasped her hands in front of her. "She loves working with you too. So much so that I'm afraid she's overdoing it."

"Oh . . . I see."

"And that's why I'm cutting back her hours starting tomorrow."

"I understand."

"I'm tempted to put my foot down altogether. It was one thing for her to conceive this Mrs. Santa idea. And she can be an elf for a bit of time. But not for hours. Do you agree?"

"Of course. Her health should be your primary concern, Ms. Harrington."

"Please, Lena, call me Camilla."

Lena nodded.

"Naturally, she'll be upset about not getting to work more." Camilla shook her head. "I honestly don't know what to do. I know she loves you and being with the children. But she's fragile too. And what if she catches something from one of them?"

"That is a concern."

"But it's also important to keep her spirits up," Camilla continued. "I know that."

"What if she kept working three hours a day but took more breaks?"

Camilla seemed to think about this. "Perhaps that would help."

"Or what if we added another elf?" Lena smiled. "I just had a volunteer of sorts. Beth Phillips wants to be an elf too."

Camilla's eyes lit up. "Beth. That would be perfect. She and Cassidy are friends anyway. Oh, that's a brilliant idea." She reached out and took Lena's hand. "Thank you so much."

Lena felt a bit guilty since this could mean less time for Beth to spend with Jemima. But Sam might prefer to see his daughter working in a department store to babysitting a child who lived at the "disreputable" Miller House, as she felt certain he probably saw it. Let them sort that out. At least Jemima was enrolled in school now. Maybe Sally could connect with some other moms who might be willing to exchange babysitting times.

"You know, Cassidy almost believes that you really are Mrs. Santa." Camilla laughed. "Or maybe she just wants to believe."

"Oh, for the faith of a child again," Lena said as she stood.

"Anyway, thank you for doing such a great job in your role. Word is spreading fast that Mrs. Santa is much friendlier than Santa—and more interesting too. I think traffic in the store is picking up as a result."

"Maybe that will continue right up until Christmas," Lena said.

"Hopefully. And I'll give Beth a call."

As Lena left the office, she felt the bounce return to her step. Not only had she been wrong about Justine spreading her poison, but it seemed that Camilla was pleased with her work. Life was good!

⟡

Life continued being good for the next few days. On Monday, Lena cashed her first paycheck. She considered opening an account, but the check was so small it seemed premature. On Tuesday, Beth came to work as an elf, but with a top-secret agenda—to lighten Cassidy's load. The two girls got along well, and Beth seemed to know intuitively when it was time for Cassidy to have a short break. Plus the children seemed to just keep on coming. A couple of preschools even called ahead to schedule field trips later in the week to visit Mrs. Santa. Then, to everyone's delight and surprise, the local news decided to do a story on Mrs. Santa.

"This is great publicity for the store," Camilla told Lena on Wednesday morning, shortly before the news team was expected to arrive. "You have no idea how much I appreciate it."

Lena was more than a little nervous to be interviewed on television, but the newswoman, Maria Fernandez, was witty and fun and engaging. So Lena stayed in character, and as the interview wound down, she felt completely relaxed.

"Maybe we'll do this again right before Christmas," Maria told her. "It might be fun for the kid viewers to hear you talking about Santa getting everything ready for Christmas."

"Oh, yes," Lena said. "No one knows how hard that man works right up until the big night, or how hungry he gets out on the road delivering all those gifts, squeezing them down the chimneys and such, or that he prefers gingersnap cookies over chocolate chip."

"Really?" Maria shook her head and winked. "I didn't know."

Lena smiled at the children standing in line. "And did you

know that Santa does bed checks to make sure children are sleeping before he enters the house?"

The crew began packing up their equipment.

"The spot will run at 5:00, 6:00, and 11:00," Maria told Lena.

"Merry Christmas to all of you." Lena handed out candy canes to the crew. "And I'll be sure to tell Santa you've all been good girls and boys."

They laughed as they left. She went back over to her Mrs. Santa chair and prepared herself to receive the line of children waiting their turn. *Really, who wouldn't want a job like this?* she thought as she hugged a little girl with blonde curls, trying to guess what she wanted for Christmas.

Lena was tempted to sneak up to the electronics department during her break to see how the news spot went, but figured it might be embarrassing to be caught watching herself on TV. Also, she was sure that Cassidy and Beth would want in on the fun as well, and all three of them huddled in front of a big screen might be a bit much.

Still, she felt happy as she walked home in her red-and-white Santa coat that evening. More so than before. In the past several days, thanks to the coat, she had been recognized coming from or going to work. At first she'd felt uneasy when asked if she really was Mrs. Santa. She always said yes, but she drew the line at signing autographs. When asked why not, she'd said that Santa had a strict policy about this ever since someone had tried to sell one of his signatures on eBay last year. Of course, that had made the parents laugh.

❧

As Lena entered the store on Thursday, she felt something in the air. Everything looked the same—the gold and silver Christmas tree, the neat racks and shelves. It sounded the same with

"The Twelve Days of Christmas" now playing. It even smelled the same, a mixture of perfume and fabric. Still, she could feel it beneath her skin—something was different . . . something was wrong. She was about to ride the escalator down to the basement when, once again, she was met by Camilla.

"We need to talk," she said in a no-nonsense tone, nodding upward. Again Lena followed her up to the third floor. Although her heart was pounding with anxiety and she feared that last night's news story had somehow revealed her true identity, Lena told herself that this was probably nothing. Just her overactive imagination looking for trouble again. Unless it was about Cassidy. Once the office door was closed, Lena immediately inquired about her.

"Cassidy is okay . . . well, as okay as can be expected once she hears the news."

"The news?"

Camilla went to her desk and held up what appeared to be a handwritten letter. Then she picked up Lena's job application. "An acquaintance of yours—Justine Grant—wrote a letter to inform the store that our own Mrs. Santa is actually an ex-con with a felon record."

Lena sank into a leather chair.

"And when I checked on your application, sure enough, I noticed a little note on the back . . . with an asterisk that had been overlooked."

Lena felt sick.

"I still couldn't believe it. I didn't want to believe it. So I did some online checking. And sure enough, your name showed up in a nasty little embezzlement scandal. Exactly like Ms. Grant's letter described. And another thing. Ms. Grant threatened to take her story to the press if you continued here as Mrs. Santa. She made it clear that it would make a very good story. And she's right. It would make a great story. For the press anyway. Not for this store. A story like that would probably be the final death blow for Harrington's."

Lena felt her cheeks grow hot and her eyes fill with tears. She wanted to stand up and defend herself, to somehow speak the truth and make Camilla believe it. But she knew it was hopeless—she'd been unable to defend herself before when it really mattered, so how could she possibly do it now? She wanted to turn and run, yet she just sat there with her head hanging as if she really were guilty.

"I'll have to let you go, of course." Camilla's voice was stiff and cold.

"Of course." Lena still didn't look up.

"This is very humiliating for Harrington's. Just what we don't need right now."

"I'm sorry." Finally Lena lifted her head. "But I can explain if you'll—"

"All I want you to explain is how I will tell Cassidy." Her voice was like cold steel and her eyes were like fireballs ready to burn right through Lena. "How will I tell my daughter that her dream about Mrs. Santa and her thrill at finding you, spending time with you, believing all your stories . . . How will I tell her it was all just a lie?"

"Do you want me to talk to her?"

"No!" She slammed her hand and the paperwork down on her desk with a loud bang. "I forbid you to speak to my daughter ever again. And don't ever step foot in this store again or I will have you arrested. Do you understand?"

"But what will you—"

"You are dismissed. Your check will be mailed to you. Please, leave!"

With tears in her eyes, Lena reached for the doorknob and rushed out. There waiting outside of Camilla's office was

Sam. For a brief crazy moment, she thought he was there for her—perhaps to help her out or give legal advice.

"Oh, Sam!" Camilla grabbed his hands. "Thank you for coming so quickly."

"What's going on? Is it Cassidy?" His eyes were creased with concern. They embraced and he assured her that everything would be okay. That was all Lena could hear as she turned and ran from them. Instead of using the escalator, she headed for the stairway where no one would see her. Dashing out the back door, she ran all the way back to Miller House.

"Hey, hey," TJ said when she ran up the steps to the porch. "It's Mrs. Santa. I saw you on TV last night and couldn't believe my eyes. What's Santa bringing me for Christmas?"

But she shot past him and through the lobby, where Lucy also made a Mrs. Santa comment. She ran up the stairs and into her room, where she sank onto her knees by her bed and cried. She wished she could pray. But what would be the use? If this was how things were going to continue to go, why should she even bother?

She had known it was useless to try to escape her past. Yet she'd allowed herself to be tricked again—slowly reeled in—until she had almost believed she was going to make it. Playing Mrs. Santa . . . being interviewed on television . . . imagining that she could have a real life . . . possibly even touch the lives of others. What a fool she had been. What a silly, pompous little fool.

Pride comes before a fall. She heard her father's voice in the back of her mind. Once again it seemed he was right. *As soon as you think you're on top, you get knocked down. Knocked down and stomped on.* What she needed to do was get out of here—and fast. Before she brought any more humiliation on herself or others. She cringed to think of what

Cassidy would say . . . or Beth . . . or Sally and Jemima. No, the best thing was to get away quickly.

She opened her purse to count out her cash. After splurging with her first paycheck—buying new pajamas for Jemima as well as a few groceries and a cheap wristwatch for herself, she had just under a hundred dollars left. Enough to get her to a new town perhaps. But what then? She wouldn't even have a place to live. And to get a job two weeks before Christmas? Not likely. Still, it might be better to be homeless and unknown somewhere else than to stay here.

Oh, why had it gone like this? What could she have done differently?

She thought about how she'd filled out the job application—that silly asterisk idea. Why hadn't she just been forthcoming with the truth? Because she knew it would've stopped her from getting hired—and she'd needed the job.

But what if she'd attempted to explain her situation to Camilla right at the beginning, that day in her office? Would that have prevented this? She would never know.

Lena paced back and forth in her room the same way she used to do in prison. Really, it wasn't much different. Once again she was trapped, snared like before . . . sucked in by her own stupidity.

By midafternoon, Lena vaguely wondered if Harrington's would find another Mrs. Santa to replace her. For the children's sake, she hoped so. And she hoped it would be a good one. Maybe Cassidy had worked her magic and someone special was already in the basement with dozens of children squirming in line at the North Pole. Hopefully the little ones with preschool field trips scheduled wouldn't be disappointed either.

Thinking of the children made her sad. She missed their innocent smiles and bright-eyed, expectant faces. She missed their quiet confessions and secret wishes. She even missed the ornery ones who questioned her identity and wanted to know why Santa hadn't come himself. Perhaps she missed them the most.

She also missed Cassidy and felt concerned that this unfortunate turn of events might be hard on the sincere young girl. But Camilla seemed a levelheaded woman and she obviously loved her daughter—surely she'd find a way to soften the blow. Lena hoped so. She wished Cassidy could know the truth—that Lena hadn't really done anything wrong. Well, other than that asterisk business, which was just plain dumb. But she wished Cassidy could be assured that her Mrs.

Santa idea had been sort of inspired after all, and that Lena actually had felt like Mrs. Santa. And that playing that role had begun to heal something deep inside her. She wished she could thank Cassidy somehow.

But she would respect Camilla's edict and never step foot in Harrington's again . . . never see her daughter again. She didn't even blame Camilla. Not really.

Pacing again, Lena continued to search for an answer. Some solution to her messed-up life. But no matter how hard she thought, there seemed to be no way out. Her life, unlike math and numbers, never seemed to add up right anymore. In fact, at this moment being in prison seemed preferable to suffering the pain she'd experienced while on the outside.

For a moment she even considered really breaking a law—like robbing a bank—so she could go back. Of course, she knew that was crazy, and she could just imagine the headlines: "Mrs. Santa Arrested in Bank Heist." But she also realized this might be how some other ex-cons felt—like what was the use? As if she still had a ball and chain shackled around her ankle and yet everyone expected her to swim to the opposite shore.

Finally she knew she had to get out of her room before her own mind and endless questioning drove her right over the edge. She needed air and space. She started to pull on the red Santa coat then realized she didn't want to be recognized—she didn't want to be associated with Mrs. Santa. So she changed back into her frumpy release outfit of black polyester pants, red acrylic sweater, and purple parka with the broken zipper. She even put on the scuffed black pumps. Really, wasn't this more fitting for an ex-con with a felon record?

She hurried down the stairs and outside and started walking fast—with her head down so she didn't have to look at anyone, could pretend no one was looking at her. She didn't care where she went, she just wanted to go away. She remembered the scene from *Forrest Gump*, how in his despair Forrest had run all the way across the country. She wished she could do that right now. Just run and keep on running for thousands of miles. Flee this town . . . escape this life.

She eventually found herself sitting on an icy park bench in New Haven City Park, exhausted and cold and even more hopeless. The sky was growing dusky and the park was deserted. Lena began to shiver so fiercely that her teeth actually chattered. She'd heard stories of hypothermia and recalled that it was supposedly a fairly painless sort of death. Once past the cold, the body would actually begin to feel warm and then the brain would become very sleepy, and then came sleep . . . blissful, final sleep.

The sky grew darker, and with no one to notice her, Lena stretched out on the cement park bench, letting its damp cold seep into her already chilled body. Closing her eyes, she imagined she were dead. Wouldn't that be the easy way out? Shiver a while, then sleep . . . and never wake. Rest in peace . . . the end. It seemed simple enough.

If only she could be sure . . . if she just had some assurance that she really would rest in peace. Or perhaps even end up in a happier place. But how was she to know *where* she might end up afterward? That was her main concern. Especially having grown up in a church where she'd been scolded and warned about what happened after death when you weren't good. But she didn't want to think about that.

To distract herself, she attempted to pray, but the only words that came were from an old childhood prayer. It was a bedtime prayer she would recite for her parents on nights when they were too tired to insist upon a "real" prayer. She had never really understood this particular prayer and had, in fact, felt it was rather disturbing since she hadn't wanted to die in the middle of the night. But a lot had changed since then. Perhaps she no longer cared. So she said the words aloud, over and over like a mantra.

Now I lay me down to sleep;
I pray the Lord my soul to keep.
Should I die before I wake,
I pray the Lord my soul to take.

Suddenly these words brought a small portion of comfort. She breathed deeply, willing her body to stop shivering as she continued to repeat this prayer over and over. She wanted to believe that promise—that God really would take her soul. If only it were true—if only she could die in her sleep and still be safe—what a blessed relief that would be.

But what if she ended up someplace else? What if those horrifying hellfire and brimstone sermons she'd heard, first from her father and later from her husband, really were true? What if God was angry at her? What if he felt she had squandered her life and wasted what she'd been given, and now he was angry with her? What if he demanded some recompense or payment—but she had none, nothing to show for herself? What then?

Trembling in the cold, she felt these frightening thoughts tumbling around inside of her. *What if?*

Then a quiet calm came over her. Or . . . what if—as some people seemed to believe—God was kind and forgiving and generous and loving? And heaven was real and eternity mattered? And what if she missed out on all that goodness and wonder because she'd never really grasped it? Kind of like a human oversight . . . or being off by one number in a long equation and getting the whole thing wrong as a result. *What if?*

Still shivering, she sat up and pondered this theory, this *what if?* Being a mathematical sort of a person, she decided to tally things up. On one side of her brain she listed the people in her life who had hurt and discouraged her—her parents, her husband, her childhood church, the legal system, prison . . . Right alongside them she listed what they represented—things like anger, unforgiveness, judgment, punishment, hatred, strife.

On the other side of her brain she listed the people in her life who had helped and encouraged her—her grandmother, a few teachers, Mrs. Stanfield, Moira, Sally, Jemima, Cassidy, Beth . . . And alongside them she listed the things they represented—kindness, generosity, hope, forgiveness, love.

Suddenly it seemed crystal clear. Why would she embrace the belief system of people who had given her only pain and grief? Why should she accept their flawed image of an angry, judgmental, and punitive God? A God she wanted nothing to do with. A God who would grind her out beneath the heel of his boot. What reason did she have to believe people like that—to blindly accept their God?

But the ones who'd befriended her, trusted her, loved her, and encouraged her . . . of course she should trust them. She'd be a fool not to. And likewise she should trust their hopeful image of a kind, loving, and gracious God. It simply added up. It made sense to her.

"If that's who you are, God . . ." She stood, lifting her hands up toward the darkened sky. "If you truly are loving, forgiving, generous, and kind . . . that's what I want, what I need—the kind of father I've always dreamed of, the kind of God I can trust my life with." Tears streaked down her cheeks. "And it's a messed-up life for sure, but if you can do something with it, please do. In the meantime, I won't give up. I promise you, I won't give in. With your help and your strength, I won't give up."

Feeling like she'd just fought and won the toughest battle of her life, she marched back to the boardinghouse, where to her relief, all was quiet. She slipped upstairs, took a hot shower, and went to bed.

✑

Lena awoke in the morning to a tap-tapping on her door. Surprised to see it was already light outside, she cracked open the door to see Sally standing in the hallway with a disappointed frown. "Is it true?" she asked.

"What?" Lena opened the door wider.

"The news." Sally glanced over to the bathroom. "Jemima's in the shower right now, so she can't hear—so tell me, is it true?"

"Is what true?"

"That you're really a felon?"

Lena took in a slow breath, preparing herself to tell everything. "It's true I was convicted of a felony, but it's also true I didn't do what I was charged with. But I didn't fight it either. My ex-husband was a pastor of a church, and after I was arrested for embezzlement, which I did *not* do, I believed him when he said he'd fix everything. As it turned out, he was the one who'd taken the money and then he blamed me. I was stupid and took the fall. Then he stole even more money from me. And after I was locked up, he ran off with his mistress— another member of the church who was quite wealthy."

Sally blinked. "Really?"

Lena nodded.

"Well, I believe you. And for some reason that makes sense. But why didn't you do something at the time? Why didn't you get a good lawyer or something? Your husband sounds like a jerk. He should've gotten caught and gone to prison."

Lena looked into Sally's eyes. "Kind of like your husband?"

Sally sighed. "Yeah, I guess I get your drift."

"So how did you hear about my story?"

"The local news. Some whistle-blower woman said she knew you from another town and was outraged that you were Mrs. Santa. She said it was her duty to come forward, that it was for the sake of the children, but to be honest, it sounded more like she wanted to rat out Mrs. Santa by running to the press. Of course, by then they'd found out you'd been fired at Harrington's and that made even bigger news. You're the talk of the town, Lena."

"It figures."

Sally put a hand on her shoulder. "Are you okay though?"

Lena forced a smile. "Yes, I actually *am* okay. Better than ever, in fact."

"Seriously?"

"Yes. And now I'm free to help with Jemima—that is, if you trust your daughter with an ex-con with a felon record."

"Of course I do. And Jemima loves you. But I'm all ready anyway, so I'll get her to school. Would you want to pick her up at 2:30? I work until 9:00 tonight."

"Not a problem."

"Maybe you'll want to come by the café for dinner."

Lena's first instinct was to decline. She still didn't want to be seen in public as the ex-con Mrs. Santa with a prison record—the talk of the town. Yet, at the same time, she was ready to stand up for herself and tell the truth to anyone who cared to listen.

"Sure," she agreed. "That would be nice."

By midmorning, Lena decided that if she was going to stay in town, she would need to find a new job. She knew it wouldn't be easy, but she also believed that this time God would be helping her. Maybe he'd been helping her all along but she hadn't known it.

She dressed carefully just in case she got the chance to

be interviewed—either for a job or by the news media. And although it felt like she was taping a target to her backside, she pulled on the red coat.

Fortunately the boardinghouse was quiet when she slipped downstairs and outside. Across the street, she bought a newspaper from a machine and then hurried around the corner to a coffee shop. She ordered the house coffee and a cranberry muffin. Her plan was to sit there undisturbed and to study the "Help Wanted" section.

"Hey, are you Mrs. Santa?" the girl behind the counter asked as she counted out Lena's change.

"Not anymore," Lena confessed.

The girl frowned as she closed the till. "I actually thought it was kind of mean that Harrington's fired you. I mean, you did your time, right?"

Lena nodded as she slipped the change into her purse.

"So what's the big deal? Why couldn't you keep on being Mrs. Santa? It looked like the kids really liked you too. I remember when I was about three and my mom forced me to sit on Santa's lap, and he stunk like booze and sweat and who knows what else. It was gross." She poured the coffee. "The dude totally creeped me out and I could've been warped about Christmas for good."

Lena suppressed a smile.

The girl wiped some spilled coffee with a rag. "Seriously, I had Santa issues for a while. I mean, who knew what kind of history that guy had? For all my mom knew, he might've been a pervert wanted for child molestation." She set the cup on the counter with a loud thunk.

Lena blinked. "You just never know." She smiled at the irony of a smiley face tattoo on the girl's wrist.

She smiled back. "And you seem like a nice lady to me. They just need to get over it."

"Thanks." Lena picked up her coffee. "Too bad everyone doesn't see it that way."

"Well, they should."

Lena went over to a corner table and unfolded the newspaper, and there on the front page was an article about Mrs. Santa. Naturally, someone had dug out her old mug shot, which was actually not bad, considering she was eight years younger and her hair had been nicely styled at the time. Of course, her expression was sad. Sad and confused.

She wasn't going to read the article but then reconsidered. Hadn't she buried her head in the sand long enough? To her surprise and relief, it wasn't as bad as she'd expected. It seemed that some people, like the coffee girl, thought it was silly that she'd been fired. Others, like Justine Grant, sounded like Lena should be tarred and feathered and driven out of town.

"I couldn't believe my eyes," Justine was quoted as saying, "that a woman like Lena Markham, someone who'd done time in prison for stealing money from a church, was now working with innocent children. And that she'd have the nerve to dress up like Mrs. Santa, of all things. Well, it's outrageous, and I just had to stand up for what's right."

She read on down to the comment made by Camilla Harrington. "We have a job application that includes a question about criminal history, and had I known Ms. Markham was a convicted felon, I would not have hired her in the first place." The reporter then asked if she believed that Ms. Markham had intentionally deceived Camilla to get the job. "No," Camilla answered, "not intentionally. But she hadn't been forthcoming either. We wish Ms. Markham no ill, but we felt it prudent to let her go." When asked if a replacement had been found, Camilla said they were still looking.

Lena flipped to the classified section. But the "Help Wanted" column contained only four job descriptions. One for an electrician, one for a bartender, one for a truck driver, and one for an LPN. She closed the paper and sighed. Well, she hadn't expected it to be easy. But she wasn't going to give up either. The classifieds weren't the only places to find a job. Some towns had state employment offices. Some had temporary employment services. Someone somewhere had to be hiring—even if it was sweeping floors or doing laundry.

After she finished her coffee and muffin, she cleared her own table and stopped by to speak to the girl again. "Do you know if there's an employment division in town?"

"You're looking for a job?"

"Yes."

"Well, my boyfriend's dad is looking for a part-time receptionist. He's an accountant and tax season is coming, so he needs help between January and April. I thought about it for myself, but I don't want to give up this job for only a few months of work. Still, it would be better than nothing. If you don't mind answering phones and stuff."

Lena pressed her lips together and nodded. "I could do that." She wanted to add "and a lot more." But maybe this was a chance for her to get a foot in the door.

The girl wrote down a name and number. "The only reason I can remember the number is because most of the town has the same prefix, and then it's the letters T-A-X-S, like taxes with no *e*."

"Hopefully his math is better than his spelling."

The girl laughed. "Good luck, Mrs. Santa. By the way, cool coat."

Lena almost said that it was this very coat that had gotten her into all this trouble in the first place. But maybe that wasn't the real reason. And maybe she'd gotten into a good kind of trouble. Being thrust into the public like that, forced to deal with things . . . maybe it was what she needed.

As Lena walked the several blocks over to Jemima's new grade school, she was feeling hopeful and positive. And she looked forward to spending time with Jemima again. Worried that she might not find the school or it would take longer to get there than expected, she had purposely set out fifteen minutes earlier than Sally had told her. As a result she was one of the first adults standing outside the school, waiting for the kids. As a few more gathered, she sensed the other moms were keeping their distance, looking at her with suspicion.

Finally a petite brunette approached. "Were you the one who played Mrs. Santa at Harrington's?"

Lena braced herself. "Yes."

The woman frowned. "What are you doing *here*?"

"Waiting for school to let out." Lena glanced at her watch to find there was still about ten minutes until school would end.

"Why?" the woman demanded.

"I'm here to pick up a child."

The woman's eyes narrowed with suspicion. "You don't have kids at this school. If you did, I would know because I'm the PTA president and I know *everyone*. Including Justine Grant. And according to her, you are bad news."

"You're right about one thing." Lena smiled. "I don't have any children. I'm picking up a child for a friend."

The woman looked over her shoulder, calling to the others who were watching. "It seems that Mrs. Santa is here to pick up *someone else's* kid. What do we think of that?"

The other women drifted over and started to question her, asking things like, "What friend?" and "Which child?" and "Were you really in prison?" and "Why did you move to New Haven anyway?" and just too many questions to answer succinctly.

"Look," Lena said loudly. "I'm simply picking up a little girl who's new at school—and life's been a little hard for her recently, so I'd appreciate it if you didn't make it any worse right now."

"How do we know you're *authorized* to pick up someone else's child?" the PTA president challenged. "What if you're a kidnapper?"

Lena laughed as she held out her arms. "Yes, I suppose a kidnapper would show up wearing a coat like this and in broad daylight, right outside of the school grounds with all of you as witnesses. Plus, if you'll notice, I don't have a car. So of course I must plan to snatch a child and make a run for it on foot. I'm sure the police won't be able to spot me or catch me."

"She's got a point," a tall, athletic-looking woman said. "And if she did make a run for it, I think I could take her." The others laughed, and Lena hoped this was the end of the grade-school inquisition.

"Oh, come on, you guys." A woman in pink sweats shook her head. "You're starting to sound like a lynch mob. Give Mrs. Santa a break, okay?"

"Well, I plan to keep an eye on her." Ms. PTA President held up her cell phone. "If the child in question doesn't seem to know her or doesn't want to go with her, I'm calling 9-1-1 ASAP. And nobody can stop me."

Suddenly Lena was seriously worried. Suppose Jemima had heard some mean school-yard rumors about the crazy Mrs. Santa and had put two and two together to equal . . . what, five? But what if Jemima became afraid of Lena or if she refused to come with her? Even worse, what if the PTA president really did call 9-1-1, and this suddenly turned into a sensational scene where the press showed up and Jemima's face appeared in the news and Sally's husband figured out where they were? Maybe Lena should just leave and call Sally.

"What are *you* doing here?" demanded someone from behind her. Lena turned to see Justine Grant approaching them.

Wearing what looked like a power suit, like she'd just stepped out of a boardroom meeting or perhaps a press conference, she strode up to Lena and looked her straight in the eyes.

"I'm waiting to pick up my friend's little girl."

"People *trust* you with their children?"

"People who *know* me do. People who don't know me, the ones who believe hearsay instead of the truth, well, they probably don't trust anyone anyway." Lena glanced at her watch to see it was still a few minutes until 2:30.

"Are you claiming you weren't convicted of a felony?" Justine asked. "That you're innocent?"

"I *am* innocent."

Justine laughed then turned to the others. "I'll give it to her, this woman is smooth. Pretending to be a bookkeeper, she quietly embezzled thousands of dollars from my family's church, money that kids worked hard to raise for missions and things. But Lena was so good at stealing that it took a few years for anyone to notice. Then she was arrested and convicted and spent eight years in prison." She turned back to glare at Lena. "You really expect anyone to believe you're innocent now just because you're out of prison?"

"People can believe what they like. I *know* I'm innocent. I'm just sorry I didn't have the backbone to stand up for myself sooner. In case you really care to know the truth, Daniel Markham is the one who stole that money and—"

"Oh, sure, blame Pastor Markham. As if he didn't suffer enough after what you did to him and everyone."

Lena laughed. "Yes, I'm sure he suffered a lot, probably cried his way to the bank after stealing the church's money as well as my inheritance. And then he married Darla Knight, the woman he'd been having an affair with while he was married to me. But I wonder if he stayed with her very long, or did he just take her money too? She was loaded, remember?"

Justine looked caught off guard.

"Maybe the truth will come to light someday," Lena said quietly. "But for now I'd appreciate it if you'd allow me to pick up my friend's daughter without making a scene. You seem to care about the children, Justine. That's what you told the newspaper reporter." Kids were spilling out of the building now. "If you really care about them, don't make life any harder for this little girl."

Justine turned and walked away, and the children trickled over to their moms. Lena spied Jemima slowly emerging from the building, cautiously coming down the steps of the school as if she wasn't sure who was picking her up. Or maybe Sally had warned her to be watchful in case her father tried to snatch her away. Hopefully it wasn't because Jemima knew about Mrs. Santa and felt wary of Lena. Just then she spotted Lena and started running toward her.

"Lena!" she cried as she ran into her arms. "I'm so happy to see you!"

Lena enveloped her in a big hug made warmer by the thick Santa coat. "I'm happy to see you too." She kneeled down to zip up Jemima's jacket, tucking her hair into her hood then tying the string beneath her chin. "It's cold out today," she told her, "and we have a ways to walk."

"Can we go to the library?" Jemima asked.

"Great idea!" Lena took the warm and slightly sticky little hand in hers, turned her back on the mommy brigade, and walked away. She knew they weren't all mean-spirited and cantankerous women. It was even possible that Justine wasn't as hard as she seemed, but simply misinformed. Even so, Lena was glad to escape them. Without a doubt, standing up for herself in an attempt to clear her name would not get any easier. And she would probably continue to attract enemies. But in the long run she hoped it would be worth it.

Jemima headed straight for the Christmas books in the children's section. She gathered up several, hoping they could check them out, but Lena was unsure. "You stay here and do these puzzles," she said, "and I'll go see about getting a library card."

With one eye on Jemima, Lena waited for the librarian at the children's desk to help her then explained she'd like to get a library card.

"All I need are two pieces of ID," the librarian said.

"Well," Lena said quietly, "that's the problem. You see, I'm new to town, and the truth is I was just released from prison and I only have one piece of ID and—"

"Are you Mrs. Santa?"

Lena forced a smile. "I *was* Mrs. Santa. But I'm not—"

"I've been following your story on the news and I'm so irked by the whole thing." The woman shook her head with a scowl. "It puts such a negative spin on Christmas."

"I know it sounds bad," Lena said. "But the truth is I was convicted of a crime I didn't even commit and—"

"No, no. That's not it." The woman waved her hand. "I'm irritated at how they're treating you. It's so unfair. Even if you did commit a crime, if you served your time and if you're sorry and you want a fresh start, it's wrong for people to hold you back like that. I saw the news spot on TV and thought you made a lovely Mrs. Santa. I actually wanted to invite you here to read a story for the children some morning. In fact, if you have the time, I might still be interested."

"I have the time now."

The librarian nodded. "Yes, it seems you do. But I suppose you don't have the costume."

Lena shook her head.

"Although that coat would almost work."

Suddenly Lena got an idea. "What if I did have a costume?"

The librarian smiled. "Then I'd welcome you to come and do story hour tomorrow. Saturday morning is our biggest story hour, and it's especially busy the closer we get to Christmas. Moms like having an hour-long break to get a little shopping done."

"I'll do it." Lena nodded.

"Oh, that's wonderful." She frowned. "I just wish I'd had a chance to get something in the newspaper. Perhaps you'd be available to do it two Saturdays in a row."

"I'm sure that's a possibility."

The librarian stuck out her hand. "Let me introduce myself. I'm Grace Lewis and the head librarian. I don't usually work at the children's desk, but Joan was sick today."

"I'm Lena Markham. Aka Mrs. Santa."

"And now about that library card." Grace's brow creased. "I understand the ID problem. But since I know you because of the TV news and the paper—and because you'll be our guest storyteller tomorrow—I will bend the rules. But I'll limit you to checking out just one book the first time. Is that okay?"

Lena smiled. "That's wonderful. Thank you, Grace."

"Story hour begins at ten. But I'll get someone to introduce you first and then you can make your big entrance." Grace rubbed her hands together. "This will be such fun."

Finally, with her new library card in hand, Lena checked out the picture book Jemima had selected. Naturally it was a Christmas book. As they walked home, Lena told Jemima about story hour tomorrow.

"Can I come too?" Jemima asked.

"Yes. But I'll have to tell you a secret first. Do you think you can keep it?"

Jemima nodded. "I'm good at secrets!"

"Tomorrow I'm going to dress up like Mrs. Santa."

"Really?" Jemima looked up with wide-eyed awe.

"Yes. And I want you to pretend with me that I really am Mrs. Santa, okay?"

She nodded somberly. "Okay."

"And that means I'll have to stop and get a few things at the fabric store. Is that all right with you?"

"Yeah!"

They stopped at the fabric store, and as she navigated the aisles, Lena thankfully remembered her mother for having taught her to sew as a girl. Of course, Lena knew this project wouldn't be easy, since without a sewing machine it would involve only hand sewing. But how else would Mrs. Santa sew?

Pushing the cart ahead of her and stopping to answer Jemima's questions, she soon located a bolt of red velvet that was 50 percent off. She'd use it for a vest and gathered skirt, similar to what she'd worn in the store. Then she added a bolt of white plush for fur trim, also 50 percent off. It seemed that this was late in the season for buying Christmas fabrics, and that was fine with her. Looking in the bargain bin, she found some shiny silver buttons, lace trim, red and green embroidery tape, and even some white cotton for 99 cents a yard that would work for a little apron and hair bonnet. Finally she stopped by the felt section and picked up a bolt of green and red.

"What's that for?" Jemima asked, as she did every time Lena picked up something.

"I was just thinking . . . how would you like to be Mrs. Santa's elf?"

Jemima looked like she was about to burst. "Yes! Yes!" She began to hop up and down.

"Here's the deal," Lena said as they wheeled the cart to the register. "I'll try to have your elf outfit ready, but if it's not done by tomorrow, I'll have it done for the next library story time. And that will be the Saturday before Christmas, so it will be extra special."

"How about these too?" Jemima picked up a card with silver jingle bells and shook it. "Shouldn't Mrs. Santa have bells?" Lena was tempted to pass on the bells, which were $2.99. But the hopeful look in Jemima's eyes made her say okay. Lena knew this costume was an expense she couldn't really afford on her limited funds, but she felt compelled to do it. And thanks to the markdowns and clearance items, along with an additional 10 percent off coupon that the salesclerk let her use, the total was $27.60. Not bad. Still, it would take a toll on her budget. But at least she had a check coming from Harrington's. That would help.

As they reached Miller House, Lena noticed Mrs. Davies, the elderly woman who occasionally helped watch Jemima, coming toward them, waving as if she wanted them to wait for her.

"Hello, Mrs. Davies," Lena said as she paused by the walk.

"There was a man here this afternoon," Mrs. Davies huffed. "He was looking for you, Lena."

"A man?" Lena frowned. "Did he say who he was?"

"No, but he looked important. Had on a suit and overcoat . . . and a briefcase." She frowned. "I hope it's not trouble."

For Jemima's sake, Lena laughed. "If it's trouble, it wouldn't be his first visit."

"What have you girls got there?" Mrs. Davies eyed their bags.

"Lena is going to sew a Mrs. Santa dress," Jemima announced as they went up the steps. "And I'm going to be an elf."

"I heard Mrs. Santa got fired," Mrs. Davies said to Lena with a questioning look.

"Now, really, how do you fire Mrs. Santa?" Lena winked at the old woman as she opened the door. She quickly explained about the library tomorrow and how she wanted to get it done in time.

"Are you a good seamstress?" Mrs. Davies peered at her.

"Thanks to my mother, I used to be fairly good," Lena said. "But it's been awhile. And sewing without a machine will be a challenge."

"I have a machine," Mrs. Davies said. "You can use it if you want, but you'll have to use it in my room. I won't let my Singer out of my room."

"Really? You don't mind if I borrow it?"

"Not if you let me help you some." Mrs. Davies grinned. "I *love* to sew and I hardly ever get the opportunity anymore."

"Can I help too?" Jemima asked.

"You're an elf, aren't you?" Lena asked. "Of course you'll help."

Fortunately, Mrs. Davies's room was one of the larger ones, but it didn't take long to get it so cluttered with red, green, and white fabrics that it actually resembled a Santa workshop.

Lena did all the cutting and pinning of the pieces together. Mrs. Davies did the actual sewing. And Jemima was kept busy with gluing felt shapes onto what would eventually become her elf vest, hat, and shoes.

"I guess you'll have to wear your white tights under these," Lena told Jemima as they were adjusting the green felt shorts to fit her.

"I have red tights," Jemima said. "But I'll have to find them and wash them."

"Red tights would be perfect," Lena said.

"Run and get me my reading glasses, will you?" Mrs. Davies said to Jemima. "Over there by my bed." Holding on to her elf shorts, Jemima returned with some wire-rimmed glasses. "Oh, not those ones, honey. They're so scratched up they're practically worthless. Toss them in the trash, will you? I want the ones in the glasses case. I just got them."

"Wait," Lena said before Jemima tossed the glasses. "Do you mind if I keep those glasses, Mrs. Davies, to wear with my costume?"

"Sure, but you won't be able to see much."

Lena tried them on, sliding them down her nose like a granny, and was able to look right over the top. "They're perfect," she said.

"Now hold still," Mrs. Davies told Jemima. "I don't want to poke you with a pin."

They worked until almost 7:00, and then Lena realized she needed to get Jemima fed. "We're having dinner at the Red Hen Café tonight," she told Mrs. Davies. "Do you want to join us?"

"No, you two run along." Mrs. Davies, still hunched over her old sewing machine, nodded to her little fridge by the table. "I have some leftovers in there from my lunch. I'll be fine."

So Lena and Jemima hurried on over to the café, where

Lena quickly explained to Sally why they were running so late.

"Don't worry," Sally assured her. "This isn't a school night. Jemima can stay up later than usual if you want." She winked at Lena. "And if she sleeps in a little later in the morning, I won't mind a bit since I don't work until ten tomorrow."

Jemima told her mom about getting to be an elf and Sally laughed. "Great, I suppose I'll have to splurge on a disposable camera. This ought to be good."

By the time Lena and Jemima got back to Miller House, Mrs. Davies was nearly finished with the sewing. "About all that's left is the handwork now," she told Lena as she shook out the long, full skirt, causing the white fur trim around the hem to shed a bit. "The vest needs the buttons and button-holes. And we need some elastic through the casing on the cap . . . and a few other things." The three of them worked for a while, but as it got close to 9:00, Lena knew it was time to get Jemima to bed.

"Thank you so much," Lena told Mrs. Davies as they carefully folded the finished garments, placing them in the fabric store bags. "I'm sure I couldn't have done it without you."

Mrs. Davies chuckled. "You might've done it, but you'd have been sewing clear into the wee hours of the morning."

"I wanted to ask you about the man you saw earlier," Lena said as Jemima was heading out the door. "Do you recall what he looked like?"

Mrs. Davies frowned. "Well, I'd venture he was probably around fifty. Looked like a businessman. About six feet tall. Serious expression. Sound like anyone you know?"

"I'm not sure," she said. But the disturbing truth was it sounded a bit like her ex-husband. Why would Daniel be looking for her?

Lena pushed thoughts of Daniel from her mind as she followed Jemima up the staircase. She couldn't believe the Mrs. Santa costume was nearly finished. She'd have to do something special to show her appreciation to Mrs. Davies.

Jemima brushed her teeth then got into her pajamas while Lena hunted down the missing red tights, promising to wash them and hang them by the heat register in her room.

"Sunshine's water looks a little cloudy," Lena observed. "Should we change it?"

"How about if I fill the bucket before I go to bed and we'll do it tomorrow."

Finally it was 9:30 and nearly time for Sally to come home. Jemima was tucked into her rollaway bed, but she still wanted Lena to read her the Christmas book they'd brought home from the library. Though tired, Lena agreed. She pulled the chair next to Jemima's bed and opened the picture book. To her surprise, it was another kind of *'Twas the Night Before Christmas* story.

"This book is about the very first Christmas," she told Jemima. "The night when Jesus was born. But it's got the exact same kind of rhythm as the other story." She began to read, using the same sort of lilting and dramatic tones as she did when reciting the other poem.

"I like this one even better than the other story," Jemima said after Lena closed the book.

"So do I," Lena admitted. "It's nice to remember how Jesus was born in a stable with the animals and shepherds and that star shining brightly."

"But I still like the Saint Nicholas story too."

"Me too." Lena kissed Jemima good night and turned off the light. "Now go to sleep, little elf. We have a big day tomorrow."

After Sally got home, Lena filled the fish bucket with water and washed out Jemima's red tights. Finally she returned to her room and the last bit of sewing. She attached the ribbons and bells that would hang from the vest and put bells on Jemima's elf hat. Their costumes had really turned out nicely, and the frilly white "old lady" blouse that Moira had given her looked perfect beneath the vest.

Lena laid out her clothes as well as the red shoes, which might've been a bit over the top for Mrs. Santa, but why wouldn't Mrs. Claus love good shoes?

Lena set the picture book from the library by her purse. She'd decided to read it for story time tomorrow. Not expected, perhaps, but it might do children good to hear what Christmas was really about.

✁

"I'm so excited," Jemima said as she finished up her instant oatmeal and milk. They'd eaten breakfast in the shared kitchen downstairs, and as Lena replaced the quart of milk in the fridge, she was impressed that no one had touched it. But then she'd marked it with Jemima's name. It seemed the tenants respected children.

Lena put their bowls and spoons in the dishwasher then wiped down the table. "Time to go," she announced. As they passed through the foyer of the boardinghouse, several tenants, including Mrs. Davies, stopped to admire their outfits.

"Here comes Mrs. Santa," TJ said. "And her little elf too."

"Don't you two look cute," Mrs. Davies said. "Spin around, Lena, I want to see how far that skirt can swirl."

Lena laid her coat and purse on a chair and obliged her, and everyone clapped.

"Who knew we had celebrities living here?" Lucy said. "Did you see today's paper, Lena?"

"No." Lena gathered her things.

"You're quite the town controversy." Lucy held up the paper. "You should see the editorials."

"Oh." Lena shrugged. "Well, Jemima, we should get go—"

"Wait," Sally called as she rushed down the stairs with her disposable camera. "I want some pictures first." So Mrs. Santa and her elf posed, and finally they were on their way.

As they walked through town, a number of people stopped and looked, and some even commented. Mostly the comments were positive and fun. And if they weren't, Lena, in an attempt to avoid trouble, stayed right in her Mrs. Santa character.

At the library, they were met by Grace. She shuffled them into a back room where they made adjustments to their costumes and Lena switched from the short black boots to the red shoes.

"Oh, you two look perfect," Grace told them. "Thank you so much for doing this on such short notice. Our children's librarian is doing the first story, then she'll introduce you and you take it from there. Does that sound okay?"

"Sounds lovely." Lena smiled.

Before long, Mrs. Santa and Jemima Elf made their way through the library. The bells on the vest raised a few heads, but these were followed with smiles when patrons saw who was passing their way.

"And here she is, boys and girls," a young woman said. "Mrs. Santa!"

The kids looked her direction and clapped enthusiastically.

"And it looks like she's brought one of her elves along too."

With the picture book tucked under her arm, Mrs. Santa sat in the large rocker. "Why don't you sit right here," she said to her elf. Then she turned to the children, taking in their expectant faces. "Good morning, boys and girls," she said. "I'm so happy to see you this morning. And do you know what?" She waited for their responses, which were varied. "It's just ten days until Christmas." She held up both hands with fingers spread. "That means Santa has to be really, really busy. And that's why he asked me to come visit you instead of him."

"Are you *really* Mrs. Santa?" a boy asked.

She held her hands out, palms up. "What do you think?" Several children responded in the affirmative and she continued. "My husband, Mr. Claus, asked me to tell you something." Again they responded. "He wants to know if you've been being good. Raise your hand if you've been good." She waited as hands waved in the air. "Now, put your hands down. Santa also asked if any of you have been bad. Raise your hands if you've been bad." No one raised a hand. "Oh, really?" She looked at their guilty faces. "No one has been bad?"

A little girl with short brown hair timidly raised a hand. "I was bad," she confessed.

Mrs. Santa nodded. "What did you do?"

"I was mean to my brother."

She smiled. "Well, I have a little secret to tell you," she said quietly. "Santa knows that all children are naughty sometimes. And he understands that it's not possible to be good and nice *all* of the time. Sometimes we're tired or hungry or just plain cranky and we can't help but be naughty. Isn't that right?"

Now they were all nodding and agreeing, and several more confessions erupted. "Mostly Santa wants you to try your best," she continued. "When you make a mistake, be honest about it. And if you hurt someone, tell them you're sorry. That's what makes Santa happiest. Because he knows that no one can be good *all* of the time. Right?"

"Right!" they shouted back.

Next she led them in a couple of Christmas songs—"Jingle Bells" and "Rudolph the Red-Nosed Reindeer." Then she told them about how Santa was busy finishing up making and wrapping presents and how he had to check his maps, plan his route, check on the weather, see that his reindeer were in tip-top shape, and oh, so many things.

"It's such a busy time at the North Pole." She sighed as if tired. "It was actually rather nice that I could get away for a little break." She picked up the book. "And having this break allowed me to take time to remember what Christmas is really all about. Because sometimes we get so busy trying to get everything done that we forget." She asked if any of them knew what Christmas was really supposed to be about. As expected, she got a variety of answers pelted at her, including "Santa Claus," "toys," "reindeer," and "snow," and even a "baby Jesus" was called out.

"Well, some people might not realize that Santa and I know the real meaning of Christmas, and that we take time to remember why this is such a special time. That's why I chose this book to read today." She started to read in a quiet yet dramatic tone.

> 'Twas the night before Christmas when all through the
>   stable
> Not a creature was stirring, though plenty were able.
> The ox and the cow and the goat and the sheep,
> All comfy and cozy, had drifted to sleep.

She pointed to the animals in the illustration. "See the cow and chickens and sheep all fast asleep?" The children listened attentively as she continued with the tale—how the animals all woke up and their calm, quiet stable got a little crazy, how the baby was born, and how the shepherds and wise men came. Finally, the last page:

But back in the stable, the critters were awed
To know that this child was the true Son of God!
And so they bowed down, and worshiped the King,
And in their own way, sweet praises did ring.
To Jesus they sang, so real and so right:
"A blessed Christmas to all, and to all a good night!"

She smiled as she closed the book. "That, boys and girls, is the real reason we celebrate Christmas." They all nodded as if soaking this in. "And that is why Santa asked me to come here and talk to you, to remind you about Jesus's birthday. Because remember what I told you earlier about how it's impossible to be good all of the time?"

She was answered with a few yeses and nods. "God understands that. And that's why he sent his Son to forgive us and to teach us to forgive others. Doesn't it feel good when someone forgives you for making a mistake?" More nods and yeses. "So Santa and I want you to remember that when you're thinking about Christmas." Then she held out her arms and called out, "Merry Christmas to all, and to all a good day!"

As she stood to make her way past the children, she noticed a number of adults on the perimeter. A few cameras flashed. Thankful that Jemima's large elf hat completely covered her hair and hung down almost to her nose, Lena took her hand and led her away.

CHAPTER
14

As Mrs. Santa and Jemima Elf made their way out of the children's section, a tall, angular woman with a dark scowl stopped them. "What do you think you're doing, reading a book like that in a *public* library?"

Lena blinked. "I was invited to read a Christmas story. The story I chose was about the very first Christmas."

"But this is a *public* library. Don't tell me you've never heard about the separation of church and state."

Lena held up her hands. "I'm not from a church."

"But you're preaching."

"I was reading a children's book."

"About *Jesus*." She spat the name as if it left a foul taste in her mouth.

Lena nodded. "Jesus's birth is why we celebrate Christmas. Note the word *Christ*mas. It's because—"

"But not all of us are Christians," the woman persisted. "For your information, I'm Jewish and my son was here for story hour and—"

"Jesus was Jewish too."

She waved her hand. "I don't care about that."

"Well, I'm sorry if the story offended you. If nothing

else, you could simply consider it a history lesson for your child."

"History or a fairy tale?"

Lena smiled. "Kind of like Santa Claus? Now, if you'll excuse us." She continued leading Jemima away.

"Oh, dear," Grace said as they regrouped in the back room. "I didn't know you had planned to read a book like that."

"It's a library book," Lena pointed out.

"About the first Christmas," Jemima said innocently.

"Yes, I know. And I don't have a problem with that myself. But there was a reporter here, and now he'd like to speak to you."

Lena agreed to talk to the reporter, saying almost the same thing she'd said to the peeved woman. After a few questions, a small crowd began to gather, including the children. "You see," she told the reporter, "children are capable of understanding that Christmas is more than just Santa and gifts. Right, kids?" They responded positively. "And too many people treat children as if they have half a brain, but we know that they have a whole brain. Right, kids?" Even more positive responses came from this. "And children like to know the truth."

"But coming in here as Mrs. Santa and then telling a Jesus story?" the reporter persisted.

"Check your history books," she told him. "Santa Claus and Jesus have enjoyed a good long relationship for centuries. Even the origins of Santa Claus, Father Christmas, and Saint Nicholas are linked to Christ and the church."

"You should listen to Mrs. Santa," the girl with the short brown hair said. "She knows what she's talking about."

Fortunately this caused a number of spectators to laugh. Mrs. Santa focused all her attention on the children and allowed their parents to take pictures of them with her. Eventually the reporter gave up and left. Still, she had no idea what kind of story he planned to write. News in town must've been slow if he couldn't find something more sensational than Mrs. Santa at the library.

Finally Lena and Jemima gathered their coats and things and were attempting a quiet exit when Beth Phillips surprised them near the front doors. "I need to talk to you, Lena," she said.

Lena looked at Beth's elf costume and smiled. "I see you still have your job at Harrington's."

"I'm not sure there's going to be a job anymore," Beth admitted as the three of them went outside. "I mean Camilla did hire a new Mrs. Santa yesterday—a saleslady from the store who fit into your old costume—but nobody likes her, especially the kids."

"That's too bad."

"Cassidy was so upset that she wouldn't even work with her. And then she got sick and had to go into the hospital yesterday."

"The hospital?"

"Her white cell count is messed up again. She's getting a transfusion today and they're keeping her for another night."

"Poor thing." Lena shook her head.

"Anyway, I thought it would cheer her up if you could visit her."

Lena sighed. "I wish I could."

"My dad's here and he can give you a ride," Beth offered. "It won't take long."

"That's not the problem," Lena told her. "Camilla made me promise not to speak to Cassidy again."

Beth frowned. "But she's probably changed her mind by now."

"I don't see why."

Beth grabbed Lena's arm. "Just come and talk to Dad, okay? He tried to find you yesterday at Miller House, but you were gone."

So he was the mysterious man. That was a relief. "I don't see how it will do any good, Beth. Camilla is the one who needs to give me the okay."

"Dad's been talking to her, Lena." Beth pulled harder. "Just come and hear what he has to say. Okay?"

"Come on, Lena." Jemima pulled on her other hand. "Listen to Beth."

Lena chuckled. "Too bad that reporter's not around to see poor Mrs. Santa being mugged by two elves. Now *that's* a story."

When they were settled in Sam's car, Lena asked him, "So what's going on, that you'd send your daughter to kidnap Mrs. Santa?"

"I need to talk to you," he said as he drove out of the library parking lot.

"I'm listening." She folded her arms in front of her.

"First of all, will you please go visit Cassidy?"

"Camilla told me in no uncertain terms that—"

"Camilla doesn't have to know . . . yet."

"Oh?" Lena studied him as he focused on the traffic.

"Camilla's number one concern is Cassidy. If you being with Cassidy lifts her spirits, then Camilla will be okay. I promise."

"Really? How can you promise?"

"It's a long story, Lena." He turned down the street where a hospital sign was posted. "But for starters, could you go talk to Cassidy? Cheer her up the best you can."

"I'd be glad to."

"And then, if you're not too busy playing Mrs. Santa today, I'd like to discuss some other things with you."

Lena wasn't sure how to respond. She already suspected that Sam might be representing Camilla legally—an assumption she'd made when she saw him at Harrington's directly after she'd been fired. Hopefully Camilla didn't plan to take some kind of legal action against Lena for loss of revenue at the store or for not fully disclosing her criminal history.

"Here we are," Sam said as he pulled up to the hospital entrance. "You go on up and we'll wait in the lobby since Cassidy isn't supposed to have more than one visitor at a time."

"What if Camilla is there?"

"She had to be back at the store by noon, which is why Beth and I promised to look in on Cass. She's in room 408 on the fourth floor."

Lena reached for the door handle then turned back to Sam. "This isn't a setup, is it?"

He shook his head. Something about the sadness in his dark eyes convinced her to trust him. Or else she was being a fool again. Whatever the case, she really wanted to see Cassidy. She wanted a chance to clear things up with her . . . if she could.

As she rode the elevator up, she wondered about Sam and Camilla's relationship. Perhaps it was more than just professional. Not that she cared. Most of all she cared about Cassidy right now. She removed her heavy coat, hanging it over one arm. Poor Cassidy . . . she'd worked so hard to get the Mrs. Santa thing going and then it had disintegrated.

"Mrs. Santa?" a nurse said as Lena emerged from the elevator.

Lena smiled. "Yes?"

The nurse blinked. "You really do look like Mrs. Santa."

"And you were expecting . . . ?"

The nurse giggled. "Are you here to see someone in particular?"

"Cassidy Harrington in room 408."

She pointed. "Four doors down."

The jingle of the bells sounded loud in the quiet corridor. When she got to room 408, she found Cassidy sleeping, a couple of tubes coming from her arm. Lena set her coat and purse down then went over to the sink and carefully scrubbed her hands in soap and hot water, humming "Jingle Bells" quietly under her breath until she was done. She knew enough about illnesses and germs to know that poor Cassidy didn't need to be exposed to anything that Lena might've picked up at the library.

She dried her hands then went over to stand by Cassidy. So pale and fragile looking . . . and young. And with the thick auburn hair, which Lena had suspected was a wig, now sitting on a wig stand over by the window, Cassidy's pale, rounded head reminded Lena of a baby bird. It was covered with short, soft fuzz about the color of a ripe peach. Lena was tempted to touch it but didn't want to scare the girl.

"Sweet Cassidy," she said quietly. "I have missed you so much."

Cassidy opened her eyes and looked up. "Mrs. Santa."

Lena smiled and reached for her hand. "Yes."

"You came."

"Of course I came. Wild reindeer couldn't keep me away."

"How was the trip?"

"Well, you know how it is at the North Pole these days. Busy busy. So busy that I had to come on the bus."

Cassidy smiled. "I like your new outfit." She reached over and jingled a bell. "Nice touch."

"I figured what was good for Santa was good for me. And

now you can hear me coming." She put her other hand over Cassidy's, holding it between her own. "You've got to get well, you know."

"I know." Cassidy sighed. "Believe me, I *want* to get well."

"I hear you'll be out of here tomorrow."

She nodded then looked at Lena with curious aquamarine eyes. "Why did you quit being Mrs. Santa? Was it something I did?"

"Of course not," Lena said quickly. "It was more something that I did . . . or didn't do. It's kind of a long story, but I'm not sure we should go into it right now. I don't want to wear you out."

"Please, tell me, Lena."

Lena still wasn't sure.

"Please . . . I want to know."

"All right." Lena nodded firmly. "I'll try to tell the condensed version." She began the story about being blamed for doing something she hadn't done, and how she hadn't fought it and then it was too late. "You see, I was so hurt by the people I thought I could trust, people I had believed loved me, it's like I didn't even care if I was sent to prison. It didn't even matter."

"Because your heart was broken," Cassidy said.

"Yes." Lena sighed. "My heart really was broken. And it turned cold and hard in prison. When I was let out of prison, I didn't want to return to my hometown. There really wasn't anyone or anything there for me. So I came to New Haven for a fresh start. A woman who volunteered at the prison set it up for me. She told me I'd find work in your family's department store, but when I got there, it looked like there was no job."

"And that's when I met you?"

"Exactamundo."

152

Cassidy smiled. "You had on your red Santa coat and those great red shoes, and you really looked just like Mrs. Santa."

Lena smiled back. "And after a few days at the North Pole, I actually *felt* like Mrs. Santa. My cold heart was quickly defrosting. I loved working with you and being with the children. It made me feel alive again."

"That's why I don't get it. Why did you leave then?"

"Well, I hadn't been completely honest on my job application. Where it asked if I'd committed a crime, I wrote this tiny note about it. I suppose I was trying to cover it up. I know now that it was stupid. I should've just told your mom from the beginning that I'd been in prison."

"But then she wouldn't have hired you."

Lena nodded. "That's what I was worried about. Even so, honesty would've been the best policy."

"Maybe . . . but I wouldn't have gotten to know you."

Lena shrugged.

"So my mom fired you?"

"She was kind of forced to do it. A woman I'd known in my other town—who knew about my past and believed I'd been guilty—saw me playing Mrs. Santa. She wrote your mom a letter saying she should get rid of me."

"Oh." Cassidy nodded. "That makes sense. Because I know my mom liked you, Lena. She'd even said she did. And she doesn't like everyone."

Lena held up her hands. "So that's the story. That's what happened."

"I feel better knowing the whole story." Cassidy let out a long sigh. "I wish Mom would've just told me the truth."

"I'm sure she wanted to protect you."

"Because I'm sick . . . she worries too much." Cassidy frowned.

To change the subject, Lena told Cassidy about the library visit. She even told her about the reporter and the angry mom.

"Just because you read a book about Jesus being born in a stable?"

Lena nodded. "I tried to explain how Santa was actually a very godly man, but they didn't want to listen."

Cassidy chuckled. "I can just imagine Mrs. Santa explaining about Santa and God." Now she got more serious. "So . . . do you believe in God, Lena? I mean for real?"

"I'll admit that I had quit believing—back when everyone turned against me and I was blamed for something I hadn't done. I couldn't imagine what kind of God would allow something like that to happen."

"Kind of like getting leukemia."

Lena felt a jolt of realization. She slowly nodded. "Yes, kind of like getting leukemia."

"Like what did I do to deserve *this*?" Cassidy murmured.

"Exactly."

"See, I knew we had something in common." Cassidy grinned. "Besides Mrs. Santa, I mean."

"I felt connected to you right from the beginning," Lena admitted. "I just wasn't sure why."

They continued talking, but Lena could tell Cassidy was getting sleepy. "I'm going to let you get some rest now."

"Will you come see me again?"

"I'll do my best." Lena blew her a kiss then gathered her things and quietly left, saying a silent prayer for the sick girl as she headed down the hall.

"See." The nurse who had spoken to Lena earlier nudged a woman in scrubs. "I told you it was Mrs. Santa." They both approached Lena. "I was telling Dr. Stone that Mrs.

Santa was visiting Cassidy and she didn't believe me," the nurse told Lena.

"You're a friend of Cassidy's?" Dr. Stone asked.

"Yes. Are you her doctor?"

She nodded and adjusted her stethoscope.

"Is she going to be okay?"

Dr. Stone looked uncertain. "She's going to be okay for now. But it's hard to give a real prognosis. What she really needs is a bone marrow transplant, but so far we haven't managed to locate a match."

"How does that work anyway? I mean finding a match?"

Dr. Stone quickly explained how a potential donor allowed a bone marrow sample to be taken and then how that information was placed on a national list that doctors accessed in hopes of finding a match for patients. "Sometimes it takes a while."

"I'd like to be a donor," Lena said suddenly.

The doctor nodded to the nurse. "Kathy probably has some information about how to join the program."

"Sure," Kathy told her. "Come to the nurses' station and I'll get it for you." She went back and rummaged through a desk, returning with a pamphlet. "Odds are against that you'd be a match for Cassidy. But you might match someone else in another part of the country. And the more people we get signed up, the better it is for all patients who are waiting." Kathy's eyes lit up. "Hey, if the word got out that Mrs. Santa was a donor, maybe others would sign up too."

"Maybe I should notify the presses." Lena was only partly joking.

"Yeah, you should." She handed her the pamphlet. "And speaking of Mrs. Santa . . . I was wondering if you'd have time to stop by the children's ward sometime between now and Christmas. You know, to cheer them up."

"I'd love to," Lena said.

Kathy reached for a piece of paper. "Call this woman and tell her I spoke to you. Maybe she'd want you to come for the Christmas party."

Lena slipped it into her purse. "Thank you."

"No, thank *you*."

As Lena rode down the elevator, she wondered how many ways she could put Mrs. Santa to use. Maybe being fired from Harrington's wasn't the worst thing to happen after all. But it would be nice if she could do more than just volunteer. It was fun and fulfilling helping others, but, like Lucy had warned a while back, Lena's rent money was still due at Christmas. And even Mrs. Santa would be expected to pay up.

CHAPTER
15

By the time Lena got back down to the lobby, only Sam was there waiting for her. "Where are the elves?" she asked him.

A young man with a toddler on his lap looked curiously at her. "You lost your elves?"

She put a finger on her chin. "Well, I'm sure they were right here when I went upstairs."

The man chuckled as the toddler held out her hands toward Lena. She winked at the child then turned back to Sam.

"Yes, the elves are gone," he said. "Jemima was getting hungry. So Beth called my mom and asked if they could come visit her for a while. Beth offered to babysit Jemima until you got back." He stood, setting down a well-worn news magazine.

"That was nice of Beth and Moira."

"Mom swung by and picked them up about ten minutes ago."

"How is your mom anyway?" It had been almost a week since Lena had seen Moira. And she'd wondered how her kind mentor would react to all that had been in the news these last few days. Hopefully Moira wasn't embarrassed by it.

"Mom's fine. She sends you her best."

"She's such a wonderful person."

"So . . . are you ready to talk?" he asked as he held the door for her.

"I suppose so." She frowned as they walked outside. The wind was blowing hard and it felt like snow was in the air.

"How about if we go to my office?"

"That's fine." She pulled her coat more tightly around her, wondering what she was getting herself into.

As Sam drove her through town, he confessed to having had a long conversation with his mother on Thursday night. "I told her about what happened at Harrington's," he admitted. "I felt she had the right to know . . . you know, since she'd been helping you."

"Yes, I wanted her to know, but I'd been wondering how I'd explain it to her. She had such high expectations for me to make something of my life . . . and then I failed."

"After I told her about the firing, well, she told me your story. I hope you don't mind."

Lena shrugged. "Not really. I'd hoped to keep this whole thing under wraps at first. You know, the crazy dream of getting a fresh start. I figured the whole prison thing was over and done with—why not forget it? But apparently that's not the way it works."

"Unfortunately, that's usually the situation."

"So now I'm telling anyone who wants to know. Well, as long as I'm not playing Mrs. Santa. She's her own character with no prison background to hide." She kind of laughed. "Maybe that's why I like being Mrs. Santa so much."

"Speaking of Mrs. Santa, was Cassidy glad to see you?"

"We were both glad to see each other. We had a nice visit and I told Cassidy the truth. I just hope Camilla doesn't find out and file a restraining order on me."

"I promised to handle that and I will."

A shock wave ran through her. Sam's words were chillingly similar to what Daniel had promised her . . . and not just once. What if she was falling into some new kind of trap? What if, once again, she was trusting the wrong person? Oh, why had she let her guard down so easily?

"Here we are," he said as he parked in front of a rather ordinary craftsman-style two-story house.

"This is your office?" She looked up at the brown building suspiciously.

"The downstairs is mine. The upstairs is rented to a couple of psychiatrists."

"That's handy," she said as they went up the walk. "You sue 'em and they soothe 'em. Or maybe it's vice versa."

He laughed as he unlocked the front door. "Mrs. Santa is a witty woman."

"Surely you wouldn't expect Mr. Santa to marry an old stick in the mud."

"No, of course not." He flipped on a light switch. "Right this way."

Soon they were seated in an attractive and comfortable office, with him behind the desk and her in one of the leather club chairs opposite him.

"Are you warm enough?" he asked.

She still had her coat on yet felt slightly chilled. Or maybe it was nerves. "I'm okay, I guess."

"I'll turn the fireplace on anyway." He held up a remote and the flames instantly leaped into action.

"Now there's something you don't see much of at the North Pole."

He smiled as he set a file folder on his neat desk. "I've been doing a little research, Lena."

"What kind of research?" She folded her arms in front of her, reminding herself to be wary.

159

"I've been checking out your story."

"Because you didn't believe I told your mother the truth?"

"No . . . because I wanted to help you."

Again, this felt unnervingly familiar. It was so similar to how Daniel had treated her, acting like he was smart and in control and about to save the little woman, when all along he was getting ready to put her away for a long, long time.

"Okay, before we get too far along here," he said, "I think I owe you a genuine apology. And not like the one I gave you at my mother's house a couple of weeks ago."

"Oh?" She cocked her head to one side and waited.

"Look, Lena, I'm truly sorry for being so suspicious. You didn't deserve that. But the truth is I'd just been winding down a lawsuit for an elderly woman who'd been severely misled and used by a younger woman she'd befriended. I'm sure I was simply superimposing that situation onto my mother. Please forgive me."

Lena remembered what she'd told the children in the library—how everyone makes mistakes and how everyone needs to be forgiven. "I forgive you," she said resolutely. "And now let's forget it, okay?"

He looked surprised. "Okay." He opened the folder. "Thanks to the wonderful world wide web and a good detective friend, I've learned quite a bit these past couple of days."

"Quite a bit about me, you mean?"

"Indirectly, yes. More than that, I've learned a lot about your ex-husband Daniel Markham. Aka Daniel Washington and Alex Johnson and a few other alibis."

"What?" She leaned forward and stared at him.

"Your ex-husband had several assumed names."

"Seriously?" She blinked.

"Very seriously. He was also wanted in another state."

"For what?"

"A number of things. Insurance fraud, embezzlement, falsifying documents . . . it's quite a long list."

Lena sat back. She was too stunned to reply.

"You had no idea, did you?"

She shook her head. "Oh, I knew he was a liar and a thief . . . I mean I found out eventually, after I was sentenced. But I honestly thought his criminal acts were limited to me. The truth is I believed I was part of the problem, maybe even partially to blame. Perhaps if I'd been a better wife or—"

"Do not blame yourself. You need to grasp that this man is a lowlife. A dirty, low-down criminal. You simply got caught in his nasty take-the-money-and-run game. And from what my mother told me, your father helped to push you into Daniel's web of deceit. Not that I'm suggesting your father knew this guy was a crook."

"No, I'm sure he didn't. Even after I tried to convince my parents of my innocence, my father still believed in Daniel . . . and my mother, well, she was too afraid to stand against him."

"I can't imagine how hard that must've been for you." Sam looked at her with compassionate eyes. "And that explains why you didn't have the strength to fight it."

She shook her head. "It seemed like there was nothing to fight for . . . nothing to go back to . . . no one who cared." She felt a large lump growing in her throat, but she was determined not to cry.

"So you do your time and get out of prison. All you want is a fresh start. And you actually do a brilliant job of becoming New Haven's beloved Mrs. Santa, and the next thing you know someone is kicking you down again. Right?"

She nodded.

"Including me."

She shook her finger at him. "I said we'd forget it."

"Thank you." He gave her a sad smile.

"But I've figured some things out," she said quickly. "Even though some people kicked me down, there were a lot who didn't. There are good people in this town. And even after the bit about me being a felon hit the news, I still had a few people who supported me." She remembered the girl in the coffee shop with the happy face tattoo. "And that meant a lot."

"So maybe New Haven isn't all bad."

"No, of course not," Lena said. "Now tell me more about my skunk of an ex-husband. Has he ever been prosecuted for any of those crimes?"

"He's about to be."

"Has he been caught?"

"He's awaiting trial in Indiana."

"For what?"

"Oh, a number of things. He basically did to another woman what he'd done to you and a few others. He tricked this older woman into marrying him, got his hands on her insurance settlement from her previous husband's death, and then tried to get into her parents' pockets and got caught."

"It's about time."

"He must be some cad to get women to marry him, although most of the marriages weren't legal since he didn't usually bother to get a divorce unless there was money involved."

"So when I got a letter from him in prison informing me that he'd divorced me, it probably wasn't legit?"

"He didn't need to divorce you since you were never married."

Lena took in a sharp breath. On one hand, it was a relief. On the other hand, she felt so ashamed. What a fool she'd been.

"One of the women he'd scammed was from your church. Did you know a Darla Knight?"

"Yes, I knew her. I found out later that they'd been having an affair while I was still married—or not married—to him. I have to admit I don't feel too sorry for that woman."

As Sam continued to read bits and pieces about Daniel's numerous crimes and female victims, Lena began to feel almost dizzy. It was too much to take in. She felt like she was drowning in Daniel's cesspool of lies.

Finally she held up her hands. "I—I don't think I can hear any more of this. It's making me feel sick. I—I'm sorry." She buried her head in her hands and sobbed, letting it all out.

She felt Sam's hand on her shoulder as he held a handkerchief out to her. "I'm the one who should be sorry," he said gently. "I dumped far too much on you. But you always seem so strong. Really, I'm sorry, Lena. Please forgive me . . . again."

She took the linen handkerchief and wiped her tears. "It's just—just a lot to take in." She sniffed. "And the truth is I've repressed so much about Daniel. Over the years it seemed less painful to just pretend it never happened . . . that I never knew the man. Prison was a great distraction. My focus there was survival, avoiding conflict, getting by . . ." She handed his dampened handkerchief back. "Ironically, I've thought more about Daniel and what he did to me since getting out of prison than I ever did on the inside."

"After today, you won't need to think about him anymore, Lena. I promise you."

"How is that even possible?"

"Because I'm getting your name cleared of all this nonsense. Your criminal record will be cleared too. As of now, consider it over and done with, Lena. You're not only free of prison, you'll be free of ever having to check yes in the 'convicted felon' box again. And if you want, you can return to accounting again." He grinned at her. "Or you can go back to being Mrs. Santa."

"Really?"

"I took the liberty of phoning Camilla while you were visiting Cassidy. I explained everything, and I'm pretty sure she wants you back . . . that is, if you'd be willing."

Lena took in a long, slow breath. "I know I should probably look for a more substantial job, but I really did like being Mrs. Santa. I wouldn't mind doing it for a while longer, especially if Cassidy is well enough to help with it."

"I'm sure you and Camilla can work that out."

"I don't know how to thank you." She just looked at him, wondering why he was being so kind and generous. Surely it was because of Moira. Bless Moira—a real Mrs. Santa!

"You already have thanked me, Lena."

"What do you mean?"

"It was refreshing to discover that you really were who you said you were. And then there was the way you be-friended my mother and my daughter . . . well, that was nice too."

"But your mother befriended me."

He just nodded.

"As soon as I get on my feet, I'll pay you for your time and—"

"It's taken care of." He put the papers back in the folder.

"But I want to pay you for your work."

He held up his hands. "Really, Lena. It's covered. If you have any questions, speak to my mother."

"I don't know what to say."

"How about that you'll have dinner with me tonight?"

"What?"

He shrugged then looked uncomfortable. "It was just an idea."

She blinked then stared at him. "For the sake of clarity . . . are you asking me out on a date, or just offering me a free meal?"

"I, uh, I was asking you out."

"Really?" She studied his face—was his expression sheepish or shy?

He held up his hands. "But don't feel you have to agree just because I'm helping you. I would hate that."

She considered this. He *was* asking her out!

"I haven't dated anyone since my wife passed away almost three years ago. Beth has been bugging me for a while. And maybe . . . maybe it's time." He smiled and his dark eyes glowed warmly. "Besides, there's just something about a woman in a Mrs. Santa suit that gets to me."

She laughed. "Please don't tell me you want me to wear this tonight."

"So you'll go out with me?"

"Well, I'm supposed to watch Jemima and—"

"I know that Beth and Mom will be more than willing."

"Then . . . I suppose I'll go out with you." Lena felt slightly dizzy, wondering if this was really happening or if she was dreaming.

"And no, I don't expect you to wear your Santa dress tonight. But as your legal counsel, I would like you to say a few words to the press—as Mrs. Santa."

"Why's that?"

"I want to straighten out the community about who you really are." He looked at the clock above the fireplace. It was almost two. "So, if you're agreeable to this, I tentatively set up a little press conference that should be ready to start any minute now. Are you in, or should I tell them to leave?"

She stood up. "I would enjoy this."

"I'll say a few things first." He picked up what appeared to be notes. "And then you can follow my lead."

"Okay." She nodded with a bit of hesitation. Once again this sounded strangely familiar. Almost like something Daniel had once told her in an effort to corner her in a courtroom or while speaking to the DA. Yet she sensed deep inside of her that Sam wasn't anything like Daniel. She felt certain Sam wouldn't betray her.

But she also knew that history sometimes repeated itself, and some women made the same mistakes with the wrong kind of men again and again. Lena did not want to be fooled twice. So she assured herself that if something like that happened, if she were being tricked, she would absolutely stand up for herself this time. She would never be hoodwinked again.

Soon the two of them were out on the front porch, and the small town press and media assembled on the lawn quickly drew in closer to them. Lena was not disappointed as Sam told them the truth. With straightforward clarity, he explained his research and his findings about her crooked ex-husband, finally declaring, "Lena Markham's name will be cleared and she will be completely exonerated. And so, New Haven, I give you back your Mrs. Santa!"

The audience clapped and cheered and then began to pepper Lena with questions. "Will you go back to Harrington's?"

"I'm open to that," she said. "We'll see."

"And will you remain in New Haven?"

"That's my plan. I've met a lot of kind people here—and, unfortunately, some who were not so kind. But that's not unlike any other town. Besides, I believe that some of the treatment I received has opened my eyes to the struggles that inmates experience on their release. Maybe as Mrs. Santa I can do something about that." She chuckled. "Because if people won't listen to Mrs. Santa, who will they listen to?"

"Santa himself?" someone called out.

"Anything else on your agenda, Mrs. Santa?" a woman asked.

"Yes, I'm going to become a bone marrow donor. And I'm going to encourage everyone who will listen to me to do the same."

"Why is that?" a young man called.

"Because a dear young friend of mine—a sweet little elf—is waiting for a bone marrow match, and I think if everyone wanted to give the best Christmas present ever, it would be to give the gift of life. After all, isn't that what the first Christmas was all about?"

"Anything else you'd like to go on record for?"

"I'll repeat what I told the children in the library today. I said I'd brought them a message from Santa—meant not just for children but for everyone, for all ages, everywhere."

"What is that?" a man asked.

"I told the children that, although they might *want* to be very good—especially right before Santa's big night on Christmas Eve—sometimes they just can't help themselves, they are naughty, they make mistakes . . . We all do that sometimes, right?"

She got a positive, albeit slightly wary, response.

"But Santa wants us to honor the one whose birthday we're celebrating by admitting when we do something wrong. He wants us to say we're sorry if we hurt someone. He wants us to forgive anyone who has hurt us. And if we remember to do that, we can all have a very merry Christmas!"

Someone in the back shouted, "Amen, Mrs. Santa!"

"And that's what I wish for you all," she said with a smile. "Merry Christmas to all, and to all a good life!"

Melody Carlson is the prolific author of more than two hundred books, including fiction, nonfiction, and gift books for adults, young adults, and children. She is also the author of *The Christmas Bus*, *Irish Christmas*, and *The Christmas Dog*. Her writing has won several awards, including a Gold Medallion for *King of the Stable* (Crossway, 1998) and a Romance Writers of America Rita Award for *Homeward* (Multnomah, 1997). She lives with her husband in Sisters, Oregon. Visit her website at www.melodycarlson.com.

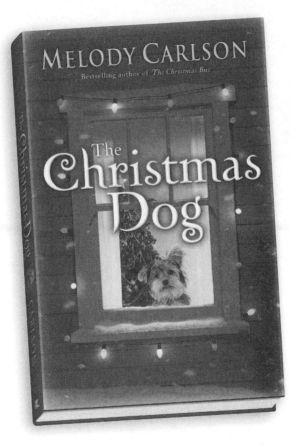

Don't miss this charming retelling of the nativity story from Melody Carlson!

Welcome to Christmas Valley, the Christmas capital of the Pacific Northwest! The people of Christmas Valley always celebrate Christmas to the fullest extent. But this year their plans are turned upside down when an unconventional couple arrives in town ready to deliver a baby.

What does it take to make the perfect Christmas?

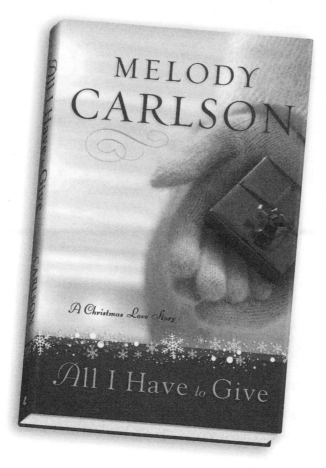

Take some time this Christmas to rediscover what it means
to give—and receive—the gift of pure love. It may not be what
you expect, but it might be just what you need.

An enchanting
Christmastime journey

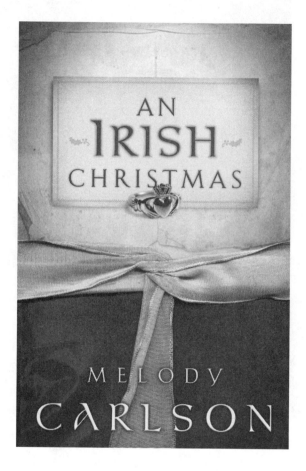

AN IRISH CHRISTMAS

MELODY CARLSON

Travel to the hills of Ireland with prolific author Melody Carlson and uncover a captivating story of love, deception, and secret passions in the tumultuous 1960s.

Be the First to Hear about Other New Books from Revell!

Sign up for announcements about new and upcoming titles at

www.revellbooks.com/signup

Follow us on
RevellBooks

Don't miss out on our great reads!

R
Revell
a division of Baker Publishing Group
www.RevellBooks.com

DATE DUE

JE 22 '11				
JE 28 '11				
JY 21 '11				
AUG 02 2011				
NO 10 '11				

DEMCO, INC. 38-3011